Kevin Dillon
June '97

'Why do you do this?' Summer demanded, rounding on him.

'Do what?' Randall queried innocently.

'Cut straight through all the polite, *necessary* little fictions and insist on baring the truth.'

'Because I'm "awful". I thought we'd already agreed on that.' He seemed utterly unrepentant, and she *hated* his grin!

So, after a spluttering moment, 'Yes, well. . .' was her dark answer. 'I now see that "awful" wasn't nearly strong enough!'

Lilian Darcy is Australian, but on her marriage made her home in America. She writes for theatre, film and television, as well as romantic fiction, and she likes winter sports, music, travel and the study of languages. Hospital volunteer work and friends in the medical profession provide the research backgrounds for her novels; she enjoys being able to create realistic modern stories, believable characters, and a romance that will stand the test of time.

Recent titles by the same author:

MISLEADING SYMPTOMS
A GIFT FOR HEALING
FULL RECOVERY

A SPECIALIST'S OPINION

BY

LILIAN DARCY

MILLS & BOON®

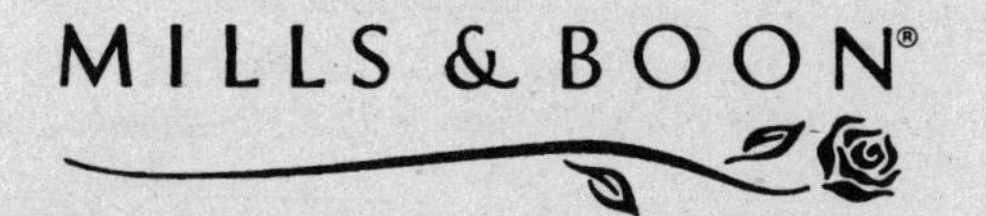

All the characters in this book have no existence outside the imagination of the author, and have no relation whatsoever to anyone bearing the same name or names. They are not even distantly inspired by any individual known or unknown to the author, and all the incidents are pure invention.

First published in Great Britain 1997
Harlequin Mills & Boon Limited,
Eton House, 18-24 Paradise Road, Richmond, Surrey TW9 1SR

ISBN 0 263 80211 6

Set in Times 10 on 11½ pt. by
Rowland Phototypesetting Limited
Bury St Edmunds, Suffolk

03-9708-50688-D

Printed and bound in Great Britain
by Mackays of Chatham PLC, Chatham

CHAPTER ONE

SUMMER noticed the coffee-cup first. Big, thick, rounded and sky-blue, it dangled from a lean, tanned finger—dangled, jiggled and swung, distracting her from the rather dry recitation to which she was listening.

'. . .And we wind up with a session on acute emergencies and long-term management, as well as the benefits and responsibilities of self-management,' Angela Keighley droned. 'Oh, did I say that was once a month?'

Summer forced herself to stop watching that hypnotic cup, and answered brightly, 'Think so.'

Not brightly enough, evidently.

'Sorry,' the other nurse said. 'I'm tired. No point in denying that Graham and I are organising this wedding in rather a hurry. . .' She patted her lower abdomen. 'And I've got a hefty dose of first-trimester fatigue on top of it all. Now, where was I?'

'You'd finished, I think,' Summer answered, trying to look down at the folder on her lap and make sense of what was written there but not succeeding.

That cup was really going now. Swing, swing, swing. Jiggle, jiggle. And the orchestrator of the china aerobics had moved into view, intent on his phone call.

'OK, Mr Scott, give her her usual amount of insulin now, but do another blood test in an hour. Yes, I know it's very difficult. Yes, I can hear her. All right, then. I know, yes.'

He listened to the man on the other end of the line, his back to Summer as he sat on the corner of the next desk—one long leg anchored to the floor and the other propped onto a chair in front of him. Summer still couldn't see much, just strong shoulders and a well-shaped head of short dark hair—almost black, except for a few silver threads.

Angela Keighley followed the direction of her gaze. 'Dr Macleay,' she mouthed, then murmured, 'I'll introduce you in a minute.'

Summer nodded. So this was Randall Macleay! He had interviewed her over the phone when she was still in London, but there had been a panel of three men altogether, in a conference call, and as she had rather nervously fielded the interviewers' questions it hadn't been easy to disentangle the different voices, let alone any impressions about what those voices indicated.

She had been desperately keen to get the job, having told John—her fiancé—so very firmly that she would not consider joining him here without having work lined up. She had wanted him to know from the day of their engagement that she was not the socialite type and would maintain her career despite his wealth. . .and then had spent nearly two months chewing her nails—dreadful habit—as she waited for an opening, any opening, with John already back here in Bermuda, vocally and persistently impatient for her to join him.

There had been a position advertised for a midwife and one for an experienced psychiatric nurse and John had already posted her the application forms by the time he'd spoken to her on the phone, only to express impatient disbelief when she'd told him that she didn't have the right qualifications.

'But you're a trained nurse, aren't you?'

'Yes, but I haven't done much midwifery, nor any psych. I could do general ward nursing, community nursing, a children's ward, Theatre at a pinch—if they didn't want someone too experienced—but I've been working as a diabetic nurse educator for two years now. . .'

So, two weeks later when he'd heard that this job was going, they'd both been ecstatic. Summer in particular, as she had been on the point of throwing aside her stubbornness on the issue and catching the next plane. She had been getting jittery at the distance between them, almost starting to have doubts. . .

'I'll show you round now,' Angela Keighley said, pulling Summer's attention back.

The latter realised that she had been staring at Randall Macleay, not consciously observing him yet somehow she had garnered quite a thorough impression of energy and warmth and commitment just from the way he was focused on that phone call. He was still listening and making reassuring interjections every now and then, evidently dealing with the father of a young diabetic child.

And that coffee-cup was still dangling. It was beginning to drive her mad.

'Do you think he'd like a refill?' she whispered to Angela.

'What? Oh, coffee? I expect so. He drinks about eight cups a day.'

'He must be bouncing off the walls by lunchtime!'

'No, because he switches to decaf after cup number two. Here, if I can get that cup unhooked from his finger. . . Dr Macleay?'

'Love one,' he mouthed, revealing very even white teeth as he smiled briefly at Summer, then he switched his attention again immediately to the phone as he relinquished the blue mug at last.

Angela took it and ushered Summer in the direction of the staff kitchen, a tiny room which opened off this main office and was directly connected to the much larger demonstration kitchen where classes in health-conscious cooking were held.

'I guess this is the start of the tour,' she said, going to a coffee-machine and picking up the glass jug that was filled with aromatic brew.

Too aromatic. She turned abruptly away. 'Can you do it, please, Summer? The smell, at the moment. . .'

'Of course.'

'In fact. . .think I'd better go outside and breathe for a bit.'

She fled, after just managing to get out the words, 'Lots of milk.' So Summer poured it out, added the milk and took it back to Randall Macleay, who had now finished his phone call.

'Aha!' he said, taking it and putting it carefully on the desk. 'Sister Westholm, isn't it?'

'Yes.'

He looked at her very intently for a moment in silence, then said lightly, with one eyebrow raised and his mouth almost but not quite smiling, 'You looked different on the phone.'

'Did I?' she answered automatically, before the absurdity of the observation struck her.

He grinned at her double-take, and spread his hands in apology. 'You know what I mean? Or *don't* you?'

She laughed. 'I suppose I do, yes.' And then, curious, she asked, 'Um, how did I look on the phone?'

'Oh, wiry, blonde, strong-jawed, boyish in a very attractive sort of way.'

'And now?' she couldn't help asking. 'Not blonde, obviously.'

'Not wiry, either. Just slim and soft, with a chin like an elf, and not boyish at all.' He was still smiling just a little as he picked up his fat blue mug, not looking at her now but staring into the brown liquid so that his eyes were hooded by fair-skinned lids.

'You'll adjust to the change,' she told him lightly, wanting him to look up again.

He did, and his smile was polite and professional now. 'I'm sure I will. You're starting off on the right foot with this brew. Angela under the weather again?'

'Yes, poor thing.'

'It's been great to get you at such short notice. She wants to leave as soon as possible, what with all that's going on for her.'

'Yes, and for me it was—'

The phone rang again and, by raising his hand, he forestalled the smart-looking woman with streaked blonde hair who had just entered and dived for her office door.

'I'll get it, Lesley. It's probably the hospital. I've had five new admissions since Friday.'

It *was* the hospital and he was immediately as focused on the call as he had been earlier, gulping the hot coffee as he listened and forgetting all about Summer.

She hadn't had a chance to finish her sentence. She'd been about to say that the short notice had suited her fine, since she'd been practically sitting on her suitcase at home waiting to join her fiancé here. Still, it wasn't important for Dr Macleay to know this. Just a piece of throw-away information about herself which would come out at some other time.

Not sure quite what to do with herself while she waited for Angela, Summer returned to the kitchen and searched for some dry biscuits which might help the pregnant woman control her nausea. Lesley, evidently the diabetes care centre's manager, had disappeared into her office and Dr Macleay was still on the phone.

There didn't seem to be any biscuits. She leaned on the counter-top a little wearily and wondered about coffee for herself. Her stomach, more politely than Angela's, said no. Jet lag still.

'Three days ago I was in England. . .' Her bodyclock was still awry and she had awoken very early again this morning. 'I'm just tired. Is that it?'

She had been so desperate to join John. . . Or had she actually been more desperate just to get out of England?

She had no home there now. It was still bizarre and horrible to think of—that her parents' twenty-seven-year marriage, which she—their only child—had always taken to be a happy one, had collapsed some months ago like a house of cards.

Her father had walked out and gone off around the world on an open-ended buying spree for the alternative lifestyle boutique he owned. Her mother was in the cold-bloodedly gleeful process of selling the small hippy-flavoured cottage in which Summer had been born in order to realise her capital share, move to a flat in town and expand her interior design business. Both of them had used Summer as a confidante, and neither had seemed to see that their mutual zest for the forthcoming divorce was shocking and deeply hurtful to their daughter.

It had been around that time that she had met John, and to be whirled into an engagement after just six weeks had helped her to orient herself again—had restored her faith in the reality of love. That was how it had seemed in England, anyway. Now. . .

Angela was back, eating grapes as if they were miracle pills. 'Sorry! These are helping now.'

'That's fine,' Summer assured her, and they completed their tour.

The diabetes care centre wasn't large. There was the general open-plan office, where Angela had given that rather tedious run-down on the timetable of classes in diabetic education, and three more private offices for Lesley Harper, Randall Macleay and the centre's second endocrine specialist, Dr Steven Berg, who was on an exchange programme from the United States.

There were two rooms, one large and one smaller, where classes and support group meetings took place. There were a couple of treatment and examination rooms, and then the usual complement of storage and bathroom facilities.

It was very pleasantly situated, however—a low, pale pumpkin-coloured stucco building, surrounded by tropical greenery, with the distinctive Bermudian channelled roof used for collecting rain water. Located just across from the hospital higher up the hill on Point Finger Road, it felt like an informal and welcoming sort of place to come for treatment, consultation, education or examination.

Randall Macleay had contributed to that impression, she realised, with his willingness to take phone calls in the open office, rather than closeting himself in his own exclusive domain.

When they arrived back he was on the phone again, in fact, but this time he wasn't reassuring a patient or relative. He was absolutely furious. 'Look, we're not talking about piloting a jet plane. He's a waiter. I don't care if your establishment is "the finest dining experience in Bermuda". Insulin-dependent diabetes is *not* a barrier to performing that job. In fact, if he ever does have an insulin reaction—I take it that's what you're afraid of—you're ideally situated for providing him with a quick dose of sugar, and the thing will be over in five minutes.'

He listened impatiently for a moment, then barked derisively, 'Patrons will think he's drunk? Oh, for God's sake. . .!' He listened again then said, 'Thank you for your time,' in a voice that dripped with angry sarcasm, and slammed down the phone. 'Bloody idiot!'

'Who?' Angela asked.

Mrs Harper had emerged from her office now, too, somewhat alarmed. 'Steve's seeing patients this morning, Randall,' she warned. 'They'll start arriving any second.'

'Oh, was I loud?'

'You could say that!' Lesley ducked into her office again as the phone rang once more.

'Well, good!' was Dr Macleay's retort. 'That was the manager of the Ocean Charm restaurant. Alan Gregory's been a waiter there for four months, and Mr Ocean Charm has just discovered that he's diabetic and given him the sack on the grounds that it's a ''health risk''. What he's really afraid of is that Alan will have a reaction, upset the customers and lower the tone of the establishment. It's *ridiculous*! Does anyone know anything about the place?'

'Ocean Charm?' Angela said. 'It's in Horseshoe Bay, part of that new Élysée Hotel.'

'Ah, good! That means there's higher-up that I can go to. I'm not letting this rest.'

'You'll have to for now,' Lesley Harper said, appearing again. 'That was the hospital on the other line. They want you there straight away. Brian Page is about to discharge himself.'

'The hell he is! Well, I'll get back to this other little matter later, then. Lesley, this is Summer Westholm, of course. You've probably got a stack of personnel forms for her to fill in.'

''Fraid so. Nice to meet you, Summer. Do you want to do them in my office?'

'Thanks, yes.'

'Then bring her up to meet the ward staff, Angela,' Dr Macleay suggested. 'Before you do your stuff with the patients.'

He must have an oesophagus of spun steel, Summer decided, watching him down the still-hot coffee in one long gulp. Then Lesley ushered her into the office and shut the door, and she saw no more of Randall Macleay for the moment.

'Now, let's see. . .' Angela consulted a large work-diary with half an eye, while assessing the traffic on Point Finger Road with the other. Beside her, Summer waited to cross as well. It was almost nine now, and they were on their way up to the ward.

Angela's wedding was set for a Saturday less than two weeks away, and she was staying on in the job only for this week, and part time at that, just long enough to provide a smooth transition. Now she was about to show Summer over the small endocrine inpatient unit at the hospital, which wasn't really a separate ward but rather a five-cubicle annexe to one of the two medical wards on the fourth floor. Having successfully negotiated a gap in the traffic, she studied her work-diary again.

'There's Brian Page,' she said, 'whose name you heard earlier. He's a familiar face, I'm afraid. Sixteen years old, type one, onset age seven. Going through a *very* rebellious phase. Hospitalised yesterday for acute DKA, and I expect Dr Macleay will personally strap him to the bed if he insists on trying to discharge himself. He's *got* to stop thinking that if he ignores his diabetes it will get better!'

'He's still trying to magic his symptoms away with sheer force of will?'

'Magic, denial, cheating. It's all three. You'll be seeing a lot of him unless things improve. Not that he keeps his clinic appointments without a fight, mind you!'

'It's a difficult age for a diabetic,' Summer mused aloud. 'No adolescent wants to have the sorts of restrictions and controls and hard work that diabetes demands.'

Then she wondered if there was any such thing as an *easy* age for a diabetic. Some might argue that later onset made it harder. John, her fiancé, certainly would. . .

'I sometimes wish we could hospitalise all our difficult adolescents until they grow up—just for their own protection!' Angela was saying. 'If he goes blind twenty years down the track because of this period of poor control. . .'

'It's a tough disease,' Summer said, still thinking of John.

'It is. Anyway, so that's Brian.

'Then there's Janey Gordon. Now, she's a nice girl. Type one, onset age five. Now she's twenty-four. Admitted in ketoacidosis yesterday, and I don't know what went wrong. She usually has very good control so she'll probably be pretty down about this. She's just got married and she wants to get pregnant.'

'She'll be disappointed if this episode delays that.'

'She's got plenty of time. I'm thirty-three!'

Angela patted her abdomen lovingly. It was just starting to swell with the new life inside her, and this was evidently the reason for the hasty wedding, although both Angela and her fiancé, Graham, had looked so happy when Summer had seen him drop her off this morning that she knew there were no shotguns involved in the case.

Angela's solitaire diamond sparkled in the sun and so did Summer's more ornate arrangement of diamonds and a sapphire, and she thought, not for the first time, It's too big for my hand. I'm surprised Angela hasn't noticed it yet. Or, if she has, she hasn't commented. I should have insisted on the smaller one. John doesn't realise that I'm fine-boned and more delicate things suit me. It wasn't a matter of what he could *afford*. . .

Uneasiness settled on her like a light, chill mist in contrast to the bright day.

Deliberately she delved into memory in order to shake the feeling, returning to her favourite moments in their short courtship. A newly diagnosed insulin-dependent diabetic, John Giangrande had been brought to her ward in

London in a state of dangerous ketoacidosis, and, once stabilised, had been placed in her care. After discharge he had come to his first outpatient session on managing his new disease and had asked her out the moment the session was over.

He had fallen in love with her on the spot, he confessed to her over dinner that first night.

'My dark, elfin angel, gazing down at me when I awoke from that coma, with a face like a pale heart—giving me something to live for the moment she smiled.'

He repeated it often after that first time and Summer would usually laugh a little when he said it, not really believing that it could have been quite that sudden. And then he would kiss the laugh away.

'Why is that funny?' he would protest after a moment, his olive-skinned face indignant. At twenty-four he was two years younger than she was, and sometimes that age difference showed.

Her answer was always hesitant. 'Oh, because. . .' I've never imagined having all this showered on me before. She never quite managed to add these last words, but it was what she felt.

Flowers, chocolates, jewellery, phone calls, concert tickets, surprise outings. Just finishing up six months of work at one of the London hotels his family owned, John had had nothing to do that winter but come to grips with his disease. . .and court Summer. And, if the former was hard and confronting, the latter more than compensated, he told her often.

Sometimes it seemed as if he must spend most of his waking moments devising treats and surprises for her, and if she tried to suggest that he should start learning to combine management of his diabetes with a normal working life she received only a dismissive shrug in reply.

John, of Italian descent on his father's side, had an expressive shrug.

It had been six weeks before he'd declared himself ready to return to Bermuda to begin work for his family's vastly successful group of hotels and resorts.

'I'll be leaving in a week,' he had said, and then he had proposed, which—in one magic moment—suddenly gave Summer a future, a direction and a home. . .

Her inner mist had lifted now, thank goodness.

It was such a gorgeous day. Too gorgeous to feel the slightest bit uneasy about her engagement. It had brought her here to this wonderful place, after all, and away from the disturbing hurt of her parents' divorce, set against the long dreariness of an English winter and a wet spring.

As she and Angela walked up the hill together to the hospital, Summer could see the lush jungle of the botanical gardens, beckoning to her right. The sky was a freshly washed blue after brief but drenching rain overnight, and the May day would soon reach a perfect seventy-three degrees.

Angela just had time to explain that she didn't know much about the third patient they would be seeing this morning, as she'd been a new admission yesterday evening, then they entered the hospital. The pale creamy pumpkin shade of its modern five-storey extension matched that of the diabetes care centre and of the older two-storey building next door, which had once been the main hospital building and was now used for therapy groups, meetings and other activities.

Inside, in contrast, the walls were a cool, soft green, while leafy potted plants and white fans turning in the ceiling added to the impression of a cool haven from the subtropical heat.

A rather clunky lift led to the fourth floor, and several

of the main ward staff greeted Angela and were introduced to Summer.

'There's Dr Macleay, still here,' Angela said as they passed through the main ward to the five-bed annexe. 'And that must be the new admission he's with now.' The door of the cubicle was open, and they saw a thin young woman in her late teens listlessly responding to the specialist's questions. 'I'm surprised she's out of Intensive Care. They must be busy down there.'

Randall Macleay straightened as they reached the bed and drew them aside after his casual, 'Hi!', out of earshot of the three patients in their separate cubicles.

'This is Edwina Andrews?' Angela asked, gesturing towards the nearest bed.

'Yes. They've just transferred her up from Intensive Care. Earlier than I would have liked, but they're fighting for beds down there. A cardiac arrest just came in. . .'

'You look tired under these lights, Dr Macleay.'

He did, too, Summer noticed, though she didn't yet know him nearly as well as Angela did and wouldn't have commented. There were some fine, papery lines around his eyes, and a dark growth of beard shadowed his jaw. Half an hour ago down at the centre, she hadn't had a chance to take in these details.

But he grinned at Angela's words and ran a hand through his well-cut dark hair, making it a little untidy.

'I don't feel tired yet although, you're right, I should be. I was in here half the night, and got home for an hour before it was time to come in again. Long enough to *look* at my bed but not long enough to warrant getting into it.'

'What happened?' Angela wanted to know. 'You're not usually that busy overnight.'

'George Stover is having his prostatectomy this morning and was too nervous to eat yesterday, which upset my calculations about his insulin. Then a tourist with poorly controlled type two diabetes was brought in after a boating accident at about eleven last night, and no one managed to discover her medical alert bracelet until it was almost too late.'

'My goodness!'

'It had got pushed further up her arm and tangled with a charm bracelet.' He massaged his temples with the thumb and forefinger of one hand, and Summer noticed the long sweep of his sooty lashes against his cheeks when he closed his eyes.

'One of those stupid things that happens just when it's the last thing you need,' he added. 'It was a bit short-sighted of her to keep them both on the same wrist. So they were in a nice panic when they called me, but she's in a stable condition now and shouldn't require more than a look-in once a day till she's discharged. The lack of sleep will hit me soon, I expect. Got out of the habit a bit since my days as a downtrodden intern. Summer—if I may call you that—you'd better sneak into my office after lunch in case you need to wake me up.'

He grinned again and Summer found that she was grinning back. Then suddenly there was something more in the air between them. A definite, distinct and unmistakable awareness, communicated. . .how? She didn't quite know. Something about that smile and the long exploration of his gaze as he took in her fine features and petite build. The way the fine hairs on her skin had stood up to attention—the way her breathing had quickened.

She took a step back and turned quickly aside, shocked. Hadn't he noticed her ring? She rotated it nervously with the ball of her thumb and found that it felt unusually tight on her finger. The unaccustomed heat here had made her hands swell just a little.

It was her own response to Randall Macleay, though, that was the worst part. Something about the way she'd smiled back at him—and the sudden surge of heat inside her.

I'm in love with John, she reminded herself. I'll see him tonight, and then it will all feel right again. This is just jet lag and disorientation, and that awful two-month separation.

'It sounds as if everything's under control now, though,' Angela was saying.

'Yes,' Randall Macleay nodded, frowning. 'Although this new lass doesn't have good enough urine output yet to start her on the potassium IV that she needs. Her electrolytes were way off last night.' He wasn't looking at Summer any more.

'Anything else we need to know?' Angela asked.

'Talk to Janey. She's still pretty upset.'

'Yes, I thought she would be. What went wrong?'

'A combination of things. She'd been getting lazy about site rotation. Filled up her last chart and hadn't got a new one.'

'She told me a month or two ago that she liked her left thigh sites best because they were the least painful.'

'Yes, they're getting fibrous—which reduces the pain *and* the efficacy of insulin absorption. She realises now that, without the chart to keep her on a strict rotation, she was probably favouring those sites.'

'But surely that wouldn't be enough to put her into DKA,' Summer came in, using the familiar abbreviation of the unwieldy 'diabetic ketoacidosis'—an emergency condition that could be a nightmare for both patients and medical staff.

That awkward awareness was gone now, thank goodness. Perhaps she'd imagined the whole thing.

'Not by itself, no,' Dr Macleay agreed with a confident nod that emphasised his strong jaw-line. 'She had a busy week. A mild gastric upset, which she over-compensated for by cutting her insulin dose too much. Then her competition tennis was cancelled so she didn't burn up the calories she was expecting, and on the way home she had an argument with her husband which pushed up her stress levels, masked the onset of symptoms *and* made her postpone testing her blood sugar, which she also hadn't done in the morning because she was running late for the tennis. . .and there you are.'

'Poor thing, so much to keep track of!' Angela came in.

'Apart from missing her blood-sugar testing, the only thing I can really fault her on is not ringing one of us for some feedback on how she was juggling it all.'

'What about David?' This was evidently Janey's husband.

'David? He's feeling guilty as heck, of course, both for the argument and for being too miffed afterwards to pay attention to the warning signs.' He grinned again, and Summer frowned. He had such an alarmingly attractive smile—the way it broke so suddenly onto his face, showed such white teeth and lit up his smoky blue eyes so dramatically.

But was it appropriate to be amused right now? she demanded inwardly, and if this was nit-picking, she didn't care.

Her disapproval must have shown. As Angela went over to greet Janey Gordon in the far bed the endocrine specialist said to her in a murmured aside, which brought him far too close once more, 'They're not on the brink of divorce. They fight a lot. Some couples like to!'

She blushed at how easily he had read her expression, but replied stoutly, 'Still, something for *them* to laugh about when they've made it up again, surely, not a source of amusement for you, since it precipitated her DKA.'

'Sorry,' he said. His head was still bent towards hers, throwing her off balance once more. There was something intimidating about his pose and yet she sensed that he wasn't really angry, but rather enjoying this little skirmish. 'I'll keep a straight face at all times, shall I?'

'No!' she retorted indignantly. 'You're twisting my meaning!' And you're getting me flustered, and I don't know why.

'Listen, Janey is so conscientious that it's almost frightening,' he told her, still eyeing her with his level blue gaze. 'This laziness about site rotation and blood-sugar testing is the first sign of anything less than a hundred per cent attempt at control. I don't want her to get lazy, of course, but I do want her to lighten up a bit. People with diabetes are allowed to have fun. That's my message, but she's not getting it.

'Even the competition tennis seems to be more something to prove to herself and the world than because she gets any pleasure out of it. So I've got into the habit of poking fun at her a little—particularly her fights with David—and now I sometimes do it even when she's not listening.'

'I see. . .'

'So. . .' he added surprisingly, cocking his head to one side so that he was looking at her through a screen of lashes, 'I guess you were right, now that I look back on what I've just said. My conduct did need a bit of explaining.'

'Consider it explained,' Summer answered at once, then added a little fuzzily, 'And it's given me some insight into Janey. Diabetes is a disease that people approach and react to in so many different ways. . .'

'Sometimes that sort of information is just as important as age at onset and family history, as far as I'm concerned.'

'Oh, yes!'

'So we agree?' he asked lightly. 'Good!'

There was a quiet glow of satisfaction emanating from

him now, overpowering the fatigue, and she thought pettishly, I hate him! He's so damned energetic and confident! I bet the woman he falls for will get bulldozed off her feet before she has a clue that it's happening. Although it should probably be tense, because in all likelihood he was married already. His left hand was bare, but men didn't always wear a ring.

Their remaining conversation related purely to his patients and a few minutes later he was gone, leaving Angela and Summer to spend more time with the four of them.

Nineteen-year-old Edwina Andrews was still too ill to be ready for Summer's help in learning about her newly diagnosed disease, but Janey Gordon was interested in everything that Summer and Angela could tell her about injection sites.

Brian Page, however, was another story.

'Brian, this is Summer Westholm,' Angela told him in a cheery tone. 'Miss Westholm is taking over from me as I'm leaving to get married.'

If Angela had expected congratulations she was disappointed. Brian only grunted and let his eyes drift back to the rented television, which was showing old American situation comedies.

'Nice to meet you, Brian,' Summer persevered.

'Yeah. . .'

'Dr Macleay says your condition has stabilised pretty well now.'

'So I can go home, right?' It was a challenge rather than a question. Dr Macleay had already told him in no uncertain terms that he was not yet ready to be discharged.

'No, we want to do some more work on your self-monitoring first,' Angela said. 'You've been making a few mistakes lately, it seems.'

'Mistakes?'

'Isn't that the word?' Angela queried gently.

But he only shrugged. 'If you say so.'

Both Summer and Angela caught the eyes of one of the ward nurses who was testing Edwina Andrews's blood sugar at that moment. There's no point even trying! her expression seemed to say, and under her breath Angela gave an impatient murmur.

When they left the hospital together a while later, she told Summer, 'I know it's hard for Brian, but I must say that struggling against his non-compliance is one thing I *won't* miss about my job!'

'What *will* you miss?' Summer wanted to know, interested in any impressions and attitudes from her predecessor.

'Oh, our gorgeous Dr Macleay, of course,' Angela said with a wicked sidelong glance at Summer. 'Are you falling under his spell yet?'

'Under his spell?' she could only echo stupidly.

'Yes. There's a bit of magic about him, don't you think? A kind of hypnotically positive attitude. He seems to make things happen somehow. Like with me and Graham. Graham came to pick me up after work one day and Dr Macleay met him and told me thirty seconds later, "You'd better fall in love with that man."'

'So you did?'

'So I did, and before Dr Macleay told me to I really didn't think that I would.'

'Thanks for the warning,' Summer laughed, with a degree of self-consciousness. 'I'd better make sure he doesn't get the opportunity to advise me on my personal life, since I hope I've got it under control on my own!'

'Oh, I didn't mean to imply he was a busybody,' Angela answered repentantly, and Summer hastened to assure the other nurse that she was just joking. 'He's not attached, by the way,' Angela added significantly.

'Well, I am!' Summer replied quickly, and held up her ring, which flashed in the sunlight.

Angela gasped. 'Oh, my goodness, it's *gorgeous*!'

They entered the diabetes care centre through the staff door at the side and the subject of the centre's director was, of necessity, closed. Randall Macleay himself was standing there in the open-plan office, gulping another huge mug of coffee between patients and chatting to Lesley Harper. Dr Steve Berg, the centre's second endocrinologist, was there as well. Angela had explained to Summer that he was here on a two-year fellowship from Boston, after recently completing the final stage of his specialist training.

Fair, serious and thin—thinning on top, too. His appearance and manner fitted the thumbnail sketch of his personality that Angela had given Summer—an earnestly ambitious man who saw his time in Bermuda as a brief respite from the rat race of medicine in the United States, where he hoped to find a research position later on in some prestigious private clinic.

There was a decided contrast between the two men, Summer thought as she helped herself and Angela to herbal tea. Randall's energy was expressed as relaxed confidence, while Steve was coiled as tightly as a spring, with deep grooves between his brows and no evidence of laughter lines at all. She got the immediate impression that one of Randall's missions in life was to tease those frown lines away.

'But the insulin pump isn't for everyone, Steve,' he was protesting mildly now.

'Oh, no, indeed!' was the earnest response. 'There ought to be protocols set up to define precisely the profile of the suitable candidate.'

'Yes, and then every doctor ought to go against those protocols wherever possible.'

'*What?* Oh, you're joking. I see.'

'Not entirely, buddy. . .' The American accent, a legacy from Randall's own years of training in the United States—Boston, apparently—was suddenly strong as it overlaid the English tones he mostly used.

'You're *not* joking?' The frown was one of confusion now.

'I don't believe any theoretical profile can ever replace a doctor's own sense and knowledge of his patients.'

'But if a doctor doesn't get to know his patients that well? These days. . .'

Randall pounced. 'Now *that's* the problem, as I see it. Let's devise some precisely delineated protocols for doctors to get to know their patients!' And on that provocative and deceptively flippant note, he took another gulp from his thick blue mug and disappeared into his consulting-room, leaving Steve with an open mouth and a painfully puzzled expression.

'Your next patient's here, Dr Berg,' said Imelda Hayes, the centre's receptionist, coming through from the front. 'And, Angela, Maya Giangrande is on the phone. She has to fly to Paris in two days at short notice, and she wants to move her regular check-up forward and get some help in working out her insulin and diet schedule to allow for the time change. Can we fit her in straight after lunch, do you think?'

'Well, that's up to Summer since I'll be heading off at noon.' Angela turned to Summer. 'Do you mind cutting your lunch break in half on your first day?'

'No, that's fine. Although I expect I'm establishing a precedent!'

'I'm afraid so,' Angela acknowledged.

'Thanks, Summer. I'll let her know.' Imelda returned to her desk.

Maya Giangrande. The name echoed in Summer's mind.

John's aunt. His father's sister. He had mentioned her in connection with his diabetes. 'My aunt's had it for years, and it's given her a fair bit of trouble. Dad says it's why she's never married.'

And yet she hadn't fully considered until now that this meant that Maya would be a patient here. John was, too, for that matter, and she thought, I must find an opportunity to tell everyone as soon as possible that John and I are engaged. I'm in an odd position here—on staff but with that personal connection as well. Surely it won't make things difficult. . . John and I must discuss it—make sure we handle it right.

That mood of mist-like uneasiness settled around her again. It wasn't easy to talk with John about his diabetes. She realised that she didn't even know which of the two doctors he saw. No, wait a minute, it was Steve Berg, wasn't it? Until this morning they'd both been just names. Dr Berg and Dr Macleay. Now she had first impressions to attach to both of them and that made things different.

She thought back to her arrival at Bermuda airport on Saturday morning, groping for something. . .

The airport terminal had been crowded. Evidently planes from New York and Boston had just arrived, filled with people almost aggressively intent on holiday-making. To Summer, it had all been a blur of laughter and tropical colour, and amid the throngs there'd only been one face she'd wanted to see. John's.

And suddenly, there it had been, a darkly tanned familiar oval beneath black hair. He'd seen her first as he was already pushing his way towards her, just metres distant, his head tall above the crowds. She'd felt her own much paler face relax and flood with a wide smile of relief and happiness and then had seen, as they'd reached each other, that he'd looked tense and wary, his full mouth a little petulant. The crowd had been awful. He had told her once in England that he didn't like large throngs.

'Thank goodness!' she said to him as at last she was able to rest in his arms for a moment. 'Is it always like this?'

'No, the Boston plane was an hour late and came in right on top of the one from New York. It's always a nightmare when that sort of thing happens. Let's get to the exit concourse before everyone else does.'

'Good idea.'

'Is that your luggage?'

She had already collected it from the carousel and passed unscathed through Customs. 'Yes, the rest is coming in a crate next week. I was surprised I had so much. . .'

'Hmm.' It was a grunt rather than a reply.

He took her single suitcase in one hand and her elbow between the fingers of the other and pulled her along in his wake, still frowning, and she thought to herself, Gosh, when he said he didn't like crowds he really meant it! They had barely touched, let alone kissed. She had been expecting flowers, too—not because she was the kind of girl who always expected flowers, but because in England he had showered her with gorgeous, expensive bouquets at almost every meeting.

'You're looking really good,' she said inadequately, as at last they were out in the milky subtropical air.

'My blood sugar's been great for weeks. Dr Berg says my pancreas has started producing insulin again,' he answered.

So it was definitely Dr Berg.

'That can happen,' she replied. 'A sort of last-ditch stand. It's called the honeymoon period sometimes.'

'Honeymoon? Ha!' His laugh was rather bitter, perhaps because be accepted the fact that this short remission period could not last.

Then there was silence until they reached his car—an open-topped, cream-coloured sports car, whose modest size befitted Bermuda's narrow, winding roads.

They cleared the car park quickly and soon gained the road that ran along Bermuda's rocky northern shore. Looking out at the jewel-coloured seas, Summer felt the beauty of the islands begin to bewitch her already, and she turned impulsively to John, laying a hand on his arm.

'I'm so lucky! I can't believe it! Where am I staying? With you? This all got arranged so quickly in the end. I feel we hardly talked. . .'

If he recognised that this was a plea to talk now he didn't respond to it, just told her the barest bones of the practical arrangements he had made that she'd be staying in one of the secluded cottages that was part of the biggest Giangrande-owned resort here, Wave Crest Rose Beach, until they could make future plans.

'I've got a lot on this weekend,' he said, 'and you'll be tired. Get settled in, start work and we'll have a big evening together on Monday.'

Which was tonight, and she was looking forward to it intensely because surely once they'd spent some time together this odd, horrible uneasiness would go away.

CHAPTER TWO

'THOUGHT I saw you wandering off up here.' There was a quiet, lazy triumph in Randall Macleay's voice as he slid onto the bench beside Summer.

She had brought her sandwich and fruit up here to the botanical gardens for her shortened lunch break, choosing this spot beside a lily pond, and had been absorbed in the study of some almost frighteningly large and extremely green frogs when the diabetes care centre's director hove into view.

To be honest, she wasn't in the least pleased to see him as she had been thinking about John—when she wasn't thinking about the frogs—trying to picture their future and trying to make it feel a little more rosy and a lot more real.

Remembering how easily Dr Macleay had read her expression this morning at the hospital, she tried to mask her negative reaction with a quickly plastered smile but either he was very perceptive or she was a rotten actress—probably both—because he immediately drawled, 'Oops! You *vant* to be alone?' in a horrible parody of Greta Garbo.

She laughed, despite herself, and only realised then, as the tightness eased from her forehead and temples, how heavily she must have been frowning.

'Well, I did,' she admitted, since honesty had already begun to seem the only possible response to this man.

'Why?'

The frank demand flustered her. He certainly came to the point! 'I was. . .thinking.'

'Then I'll—'

'No! Stay! Please. My thoughts. . .actually weren't

getting me very far and I'd just started to decide that I might do better with the frogs.'

'With them?'

'Watching them.'

'Not kissing them, hoping for a prince?'

'Well, no, since I have my prince already. I'm engaged.'

There! It was out, and for some reason having him know this felt like successfully jumping over a large hurdle, through why that should be. . .

She held out her ring to him and saw it sparkle and glitter in the sunlight as she moved her hand. There was a small silence and—was it her imagination or had he moved away from her a little? No, not even that. Stiffened? He didn't *look* stiff. There was something, though, a definite change.

'Gosh!' he said finally. 'Big, isn't it? I mean *beautiful*, of course. Big *and* beautiful.'

'It *is* big,' she admitted, then laughed. 'You're refreshingly tactless, aren't you?'

'Only when taken by surprise. Sorry.' He leaned back against the wooden armrest of the bench, still watching the ring—and Summer as well. 'I'm now recovered enough to tell you that I think it's the most beautiful thing I've ever seen in my life.'

Recovered? Odd word!

'You don't have to say that, Dr Macleay.'

'Randall.'

'Randall, then. It *is* too big. Too big to look quite real, I sometimes think, but, you see, I'm marrying into quite a wealthy, well-known family in Bermuda and big engagement rings seem to go with the territory. In fact,' she went on, scarcely pausing for breath, 'my fiancé is John Giangrande, who has recently become a patient of Dr Berg's. You probably know him.'

'Know of him,' he corrected. 'We haven't actually met,

but I see his Aunt Maya. Well, you know that, of course, since she's due in any minute. I had no idea you were connected to the Giangrandes.'

'No, well, it hadn't come up before,' she explained, not very fluently. 'I didn't want to mention it during the interview, when it was all just over the phone, but then today I realised that everyone needed to know. I hope you won't consider that it creates a conflict of interest.'

'Hardly,' he answered, 'since I hope the centre is as concerned for your fiancé's welfare as you are. It is something to be aware of, though, and you were right to let me know.'

'Oh. Yes. Good.'

There was another rather long silence, then his face broke into a wry grin. 'And I really do like your ring. It isn't too big at all. It's just that you're so fine-boned. But that central sapphire—gorgeous! And the diamonds—superb! And the setting! Can I stop now?'

'Please do!'

'Admiring rings isn't really a *guy thing*, you know.' The American intonation was deliberate, and his blue eyes—a perfect match for the much-discussed sapphire, actually—twinkled lazily.

'I know,' she told him very gravely, 'and I'm very grateful for your willingness to go to the trouble.'

'Not at all. Felt like a damned idiot for not noticing it before, that's all.'

'Oh, because it's so *big*?' she suggested sweetly.

'No, Summer, *not* because it's so big,' he said firmly.

The twinkle in his eyes was gone and a moment later so was he, leaving her quite unable to decide what to make of the entire conversation. If he'd had a reason for seeking her out as he had, they certainly hadn't got around to discussing it.

* * *

'It's typical of my brother, Vincent, to do this,' Maya Giangrande told Summer a little later. 'Sending me off to Paris at two days' notice without considering that travel involves extra care for a diabetic. You haven't met your future father-in-law yet, have you?'

'Not yet. I think John's hoping to arrange something on the weekend,' Summer improvised, assuming that they would discuss some such possibility tonight.

That John didn't seem in a hurry to have her meet his family was one of the things making her subtly ill at ease, and it occurred to her that perhaps they didn't approve—didn't think she was good enough for the Wave Crest Hotels heir.

Maya's attitude—for example—although friendly, contained a hint of something like scepticism. She was a sophisticated and attractive woman in her late forties, dressed for business in a very expensive brown linen suit, and there had been something very European in the way she had kissed Summer on each cheek when they'd introduced themselves to each other, although her accent was more American than anything else.

'It's good luck for John, I suppose,' she had said frankly, with a small smile, as she tossed back her skilfully arranged dark hair. 'To be marrying a nurse with special knowledge of diabetes. And you know, too, what you're letting yourself in for. More than he does, at this stage, I expect. Hell, I was devastated when I heard he'd got it as well!'

'He hasn't fully come to terms with it,' Summer acknowledged carefully.

'Does anyone, ever?' Maya countered on a husky laugh and then added, with a sidelong glance, 'You must... really love him very much if you're prepared to go through with it.'

'Well, of course I do.' Why was Maya looking at her like that?

Does she know I'm having doubts?

'But let's focus on you, now, shall we?' Summer continued firmly, very uncomfortable about Maya Giangrande's attitude. 'How has everything been going? I see you've been bothered by some types of neuropathy a fair bit in the past.'

'Yes, but that's settled down a lot over the past few years. My control improved which actually made the pain in my feet at night worse for about six or eight months, but I haven't had any real discomfort for, oh, must be over a year.'

'Anything else you'd like me to look at before you see the doctor? How are your injection sites looking?'

'Oh, everything's fine. I'm an old hand at this.' Again came that husky laugh. 'I switched to testing blood sugar four years ago, instead of the old Clinitest strips, after digging in my heels about it for quite a while, and I inject three times a day on a split-and-mix schedule now. My eyes checked out well last month, but if you're experienced at retina checks you can certainly have another look for me.'

'Of course.'

'My only other concern is that my blood-sugar levels seem to be gradually rising again. Perhaps I should have brought my charts, but I didn't. I increased my dose of long-acting and that made it all right for a while, but now it's going up again. And there have been some readings that were way off, which I can't account for. Could it be an absorption problem?'

'It could be. Sometimes insulin can pool beneath the skin at certain sites. Let's check your technique and the sites you've been using, and mention it to Dr Macleay, of course.'

They got down to business. Summer checked Maya's eyes and found a few 'cotton-wool spots' on the left retina. Maya dismissed these, saying that her ophthalmologist was already aware of them.

Her feet were in good condition, 'Although with this trip to Paris you must be careful about shoes,' Summer warned. 'All those hard Parisian pavements and standing around in high heels. Be rigorous about cleaning and checking your feet daily.'

'Oh, yes. . .' Maya waved this away. 'I'll put them in a basin every night for a good soak.'

Summer got Maya to describe and demonstrate her injection technique and checked her sites.

'I'm not using my thighs any more,' the other woman said a little defiantly. 'Look at them, they're so lumpy—all those hollows and, God, *trenches* in places! I'll be in a neck-to-knee bathing suit soon. Isn't it revolting?'

'Have you mentioned it to Dr Macleay? Fat atrophy, it's called.'

Maya shuddered and gave that husky laugh again. 'Any problem that goes by the name of *fat atrophy* is *not* something I'm prepared to discuss with *any* male doctor, let alone a young, single, good-looking and non-diabetic one!'

'Which is a pity,' Summer said gently, 'because there's probably something he can do about it. For example, are you using the same insulin you've been using for years?'

'Yes. I know there are newer ones out now—the purified kind and the non-animal-based—but since I'm used to what I use and I've already developed the antibodies, does it matter?'

'It can, and if you're concerned about the state of your thighs. . .'

'Oh, "*if*"? You mean human insulin could fill in all those holes? I don't believe it!'

'Talk to Dr Macleay about switching,' Summer advised.

'There are some long-term diabetics who don't manage to achieve the same control if they switch. On the other hand, the fact that you're having to increase your dose—which you *must* talk to him about—suggests that absorbency is a problem, and the newer insulins might help with that.'

Maya shuddered. 'It's always like this! I get the system down, and then it changes. I hate that! But if you tell me that there's still hope for my thighs to get rid of that... what did you call it?'

'Fat atrophy,' Summer repeated with a smile. 'It sounds worse than it looks, I think! If you do switch I'll give you a quick lesson in where to site your injections so that those hollow patches do start filling in.'

'I'm still sceptical! But more important for now is how to adjust my insulin for the time change between here and Paris. I'll be away almost a week. And what should I do about meals? It's such a nuisance! Vincent usually sends me to the United States, which doesn't involve a big time change, but with this new pair of hotels we're buying in Paris... And then I couldn't get a direct flight so I'm backtracking to New York first.'

It was complicated, and the broad plan they worked out would have to be checked by Dr Macleay in order to provide exact insulin doses. In the end, Summer had to ring the airline as well to find out at what point a meal would be served on the flights between New York and Paris.

'And of course I'll take snacks, just in case,' Maya said.

'Biscuits and cheese for slow-acting, and perhaps a sweet—'

'A juice box?'

'Juice is fine.'

'For a quick sugar hit it's what I usually use.'

'Good.'

'I'd better tell Vincent he's not to make a habit of this! Damned disease. . .'

In fact, Summer had known several diabetics who managed travel plans far more complicated than this without reference to their doctor, but she sensed that Maya was resistant to acquiring quite that degree of expertise in self-management.

She took the older woman's weight, temperature, blood pressure and pulse and noted down the figures. 'Looking good!'

'Then he won't keep me very long, I hope. I have business in town all afternoon, starting with an appointment in. . .' she consulted a delicate gold watch '. . .forty minutes.'

'You'll just make it, I think,' Summer said.

'Provided I can park. By the way, how are you getting about? You're staying at Rose Beach, where I have a flat. . .'

'Bus,' Summer answered.

Maya looked frankly horrified. 'You're joking! John's not giving you a hotel car to use?'

'We haven't discussed it yet.' What *have* we discussed? I wonder.

'You can't possibly catch the *bus*!'

Summer forbore to mention that she had been catching buses for most of her life—that or riding bicycles, starting at the age of ten months strapped to a wildly colourful baby-seat on her mother's rear carrier—and had caught the bus here this morning, in fact, and had found it quite a pleasant meander in one of the noisy Bermuda-pink vehicles.

Maya went on briskly, 'Look, I'll be heading back to Rose Beach at about five. I'll pick you up. John's got to do better than this!'

Summer accepted the offer willingly enough. Was there

such a thing as an aunt-in-law? If so then Maya would soon be it. Then she sent her in to Randall, and heard her say as the door to his office closed between them, 'Having to see *you* beforehand makes this trip to Paris into nothing but a chore, I'm afraid, Dr Macleay!'

Patient appointments and phone consultations took up the rest of the afternoon. Angela had gone, leaving all of this to fall on Summer's shoulders, but it was familiar work and as there were no classes scheduled today she handled it all easily. So easily, in fact, that by four she had nothing left to do, and Lesley Harper had her collating and stapling a stack of the questionnaires used to assess a new patient's understanding of diabetes in order to assign them to the appropriate class.

Randall Macleay raised his eyebrows when he emerged from his office, blue mug in hand, and saw her at the task. 'Is this the best use we can make of a highly trained member of staff? Imelda?'

He turned to the Bermudian receptionist, who replied with laconic apology, 'Taking my kids to the dentist,' as she picked up her bag.

The manager was the next target for his indignant appeal. 'Lesley! We'll get our budget cut if you're not careful. Haven't I told you that everyone's to look harried and overworked at every possible opportunity? What if Max Haddy from Personnel drops by?'

'You know perfectly well that this is the quietest day we've had in a good four weeks, Randall,' Lesley replied mildly. 'Do you think that refilling your coffee-mug would be a more appropriate allocation of resources?'

'Well, no, I was planning on doing that myself, but if you want to, Summer. . .'

'Not until I've finished this,' she answered very firmly, rather enjoying the mechanical task of gathering, stacking and stapling. Enjoying Randall Macleay too.

He groaned in torment, rolling his well-shaped head back. 'Another management lackey, putting administration ahead of patient welfare.'

'*Patient* welfare?' Lesley challenged.

'Patient welfare, doctor welfare. Same thing. What is that pile of junk, anyway?'

'It's the diabetes education pre-test,' Lesley replied patiently. 'And you wrote it yourself, Randall.'

'Oh. So I did. Carry on, then, Summer.'

'I intend to.'

'In which case, could I make *you* a cup?'

'No thanks!'

'You drink far too much of the stuff, Randall,' Lesley came in.

'I know.' He edged guiltily towards the kitchen. 'I'm going to cut down to six cups. It doesn't set a good example for my patients, does it?'

'Nobody's perfect,' Lesley soothed.

'But diabetics have to be,' he capped. 'But, no, I am cutting down.'

'Why not just get a smaller mug?' Summer suggested. The blue china thing was jiggling on the end of his finger again, half the size of an Elizabethan chamber-pot.

Randall looked horrified. 'But I love my mug!' His free hand came up to shield it protectively.

'We know!' Lesley said, cocking her rather closely cropped mid-blonde head to one side so that her big, colourful earrings jangled.

'I fail to see how that could be a problem for you, Lesley,' Randall replied.

'Believe me, it is. You'll learn to dread the very sight of it, Summer. I've been sorely tempted at times to let it accidentally *slip*. . .'

'All right! This is a conspiracy! This mug is not leaving my possession again!'

He disappeared into the kitchen, still spluttering indignantly, and Summer went on with her collating and stapling, not fully aware that she was smiling until he emerged again and caught her at it—watching her rather intently for a few moments before she became aware of it and lifted her gaze to meet his.

'When you've finished,' he said, 'and when I've finished. . .' he gulped some coffee '. . .I'm heading up to the hospital. George Stover will be out of Recovery now, and I want to check the others too. Maya said she was collecting you at five so you've got a bit of time, and you must have questions. You've scarcely been given a decent orientation into this job.'

'I do have questions. About my role in relation to you and Steve. Today, for example, was I out of line in suggesting a switch to human insulin for Maya?'

'Not out of line, no. Let's talk about it on the way up.'

So they went across together ten minutes later and she returned to the centre just after five with the sense of having spent a very productive and interesting hour. Was it the coffee? Randall Macleay was certainly a very energetic and positive man.

'You're right at the end?'

'Yes, Cottage Nine,' Summer told Maya as they wound along the driveway that led up to the sprawling complex of the resort hotel. Beyond it were the pool and tennis courts and then the scattered cottages, all in soft pastel pink and couched amongst lush foliage.

'I'll drive you up,' Maya offered.

'No, please don't,' Summer insisted. 'I'd like the walk. . .and I can see a Land Rover blocking the road at the moment, anyway.'

This last reason was good enough for Maya, and she veered with alarming efficiency into a reserved parking space right outside the main building. She and Summer both recognised the cream, open-topped car beside them at the same moment.

'John must be here,' Maya said. 'Oh, of course. He's picking you up.'

'Not until seven, he said.'

'Business, then. Vincent is planning to have him managing this place within a year. Come in and let's find him. I have to see the chef and convince him to stay on until I can poach someone from Paris.'

She was already out of the car and walking towards the lobby and Summer followed, not yet quite sure about this woman. What was the source of that hint of scepticism? It didn't feel quite like disapproval. Maya Giangrande crossed the lobby, opened a door marked STAFF ONLY and there was John.

He hadn't seen her yet, Summer realised. He was standing at a desk, leaning over it to study a long computer print-out, and beside him—studying it too—was a very attractive. . .no, that wasn't strong enough. . .a *stunning* blonde in her early twenties. They both laughed, then registered Maya's entrance and looked up to see Summer too. John came forward immediately, frowning.

'Is there a problem?' He took her hands for a moment, then kissed her cheek very brieftly and stepped back again. 'I thought we said seven.'

'We did, but Maya was kind enough to give me a lift, then we noticed your car was already here. . . She suggested I come in, and. . .' Summer trailed off uncomfortably. Why did she have to explain, as if she'd done something wrong? Wasn't he pleased to see her?

Maya slipped out with a murmured, 'Off to beard the chef in his den.'

'I'm glad you've come,' John said. It ought to have answered that last question of hers, but somehow it didn't.

'I've booked us for eight o'clock at a great restaurant in St Georges so, tell me, when should I take my shot, and can you do it for me? I'm sure I'm not doing it right because it hurts so bloody much.'

'Well, perhaps you're—'

'And something went wrong yesterday, according to that damned blood-test meter. My blood sugar was 230 before lunch. That's too high, isn't it?'

'Yes, it is!'

'How about 190?'

'Still too high. You have all that written down, don't you? The acceptable ranges?'

'Yes, but I forget and looking it up is a hassle. You'd better take a look at all my readings over the past week because I don't think there's been anything below 150.'

'Oh, *John*!'

'Don't give me that you've-been-a-bad-boy tone!'

'I'm sorry, but I—'

He swore. 'No, *I'm* sorry. I guess the honeymoon's over, that's all.' Behind him the lovely blonde's pen slipped and she hissed between her teeth. 'Not *us*.' He grimaced at Summer. 'I'm going to need you more than ever now. But the honeymoon Dr Berg talked about when my pancreas flickered back into life again.'

He turned to the other woman, who was still bending over the computer print-outs as if deaf to anyone else's presence. 'Alex, I'm sorry, this must be making you sick. I know you're squeamish about needles.'

'No, I'm not. Not really. I'm sure I could get over it very easily if I. . .ever had to.' She looked up, her face rather flushed, and her green eyes flicked away from Summer too quickly.

John swore again and smacked the palm of his hand across his forehead. 'I haven't introduced you two. Alex, this is Summer.'

Alex stepped forward, wearing a smile that was almost as tight as her skirt. 'John's told me all about you,' she said briefly, then added, as if making a tremendous effort, 'It must have. . .helped him enormously to have you there when he was trying to learn about his disease.'

'I hope so,' Summer said awkwardly.

The young woman's wide mouth looked as if she were tasting vinegar, and John was standing between the two of them with all the poise of a letter box, his head turned towards Alex.

Alex who? The blonde evidently knew all about Summer, but the reverse did not hold true and John didn't seem to be planning any further elucidation. Was she a hotel employee? Yes. Summer caught sight of a smart metal name-tag on the lapel of her powder-blue suit which read, ALEX PAGE. DIRECTOR OF GUEST SERVICES. Young for such a position. Or was she older than she looked?

'We do need to finish this, John,' Alex said, still in that strained way. 'But if there's something you need to work out with—with Summer about your insulin dose, please do. You mustn't neglect yourself. Isn't that right, Summer?'

'No, let's get this finished,' John urged. 'Summer, you head off and I'll be at your cottage at seven, as we said. Then you can give me the damned shot and that should be about right, shouldn't it?'

'The timing, yes. The amount. . . It sounds as if you should see Dr Berg as soon as you can to set up a new timetable. Your dosages will need to be increased and maybe the number of shots per day.'

'Oh, God, don't talk about it now. Alex doesn't need to hear the gory details.'

'It's all right, John. Really, it is,' Alex came in stiffly. She had a rather high, hard-edged voice.

'Seven, then—OK, Summer?' John repeated, and it was

such a clear dismissal that she could only nod and leave.

In the lobby once more she felt so miserable and tense that tears threatened, and she made for the luxurious powder-room that opened off a short corridor. If anyone saw her like this, when she ought to have the same blissful glow as Angela Keighley. . .

She studied her troubled face in the brightly lit make-up mirror which almost filled one wall of the powder-room. The tears didn't show, thank goodness, although her dark eyes didn't quite contain their usual eager and intelligent glow. What she saw was just her own familiar face atop a petite body—neat-shouldered, trim-waisted. A pretty face? Pretty enough, with its heart shape—framed by feathers of soft dark hair—and clear, fair skin. *Winsome* fitted better than pretty, perhaps, although that wasn't a word much in use nowadays to describe female beauty.

What does John see when he looks at me? she wondered. What do I see when I look at him? Something's not right. . .

The powder-room was beginning to feel claustrophobic, and she heard the outer door open. Time to leave.

And there was Maya again, crossing to the main doors with a brisk click of her Italian shoes.

'All fixed up?' Summer said, perturbed to realise that it had come out sounding wobbly.

'Is it? Good,' Maya answered.

'No, I meant you. The chef. I was asking. . .'

'Oh! No, he's being a royal pain! I thought you meant John, but I see now that it *isn't* fixed. He's being horribly tactless and I'll tell him so, if you like.'

'Tactless?'

'OK, completely rotten, if you want to go that far. Alex offered to take a transfer to our resort in the Bahamas but John wouldn't hear of it. If it's any consolation, I feel sorry for *her* too!'

'Alex? Sorry, I—'

'You mean he hasn't said anything?' Maya stopped in her tracks just short of her car, bringing Summer to an abrupt halt as well.

'I— No. Please tell me what's going on.'

'Oh, nothing *now*. But John and Alex were seriously involved together for over a year. I thought you'd have known. Look, get in and I *will* drive you up.' This time Summer didn't protest, and Maya continued as she slid into the car, 'We all expected it to pick up again as soon as he returned from London—in fact, she visited him there twice—and then the next thing we knew there was the news of his diabetes and he'd flown home and announced his engagement to you.'

'Did—did he and Alex have a fight?'

Maya shrugged. 'If they did they kept it very private. I can't believe John didn't warn you. He must know that she still cares. . .'

'You think she does?' Summer managed, grasping at straws.

'Oh, heavens! She's *miserable—and* busy sharpening her claws, I shouldn't wonder.'

'I wasn't poaching. I had no idea. . .'

'I know, honey.' Maya took a hand from the wheel to pat Summer's knee. 'You're not at fault. And if you and John are truly in love—as obviously you must be—then Alex will just have to get over it. John should have let her take that transfer! He's naïve if he thinks the two of you will ever be friends, or whatever he's hoping for.'

She pulled up outside Summer's cottage. 'And now I've got to go, honey, if you don't mind or I won't get home and settled before it's time to eat.'

'Of course. Thanks for the lift,' Summer answered.

* * *

'Please do it for me, Summer.'

'But you've been doing it yourself for two months, John. Don't you think it's best to stick to your routine?'

'Well, with that honeymoon thing I was able to get by. I mean, I guess I skipped a lot of shots. There isn't really a routine and my technique is rotten, I know that.'

'Let's work on your technique, then. Where is your site chart?'

He shrugged. 'Don't know. There's no need to be exact about it, is there? I guess I'm about due for an arm shot, maybe? Now that you're here you can keep track for me.'

'John—'

'It's second nature to you! If I'd wanted to be an expert on this sort of stuff I'd have been a doctor. I just want to get on with my life!'

Summer bit back further argument and silently took the little pouch of equipment he was handing over to her. He was still in a state of anger and denial, she realised. Glib terms for a nurse to use. Harder when they applied to someone you really cared about.

She washed her hands in the sink of the small kitchen alcove, finding it incongruous to be standing here in a luxury resort guest cottage, dressed for an evening out in floral silk and performing basic nursing tasks for a fiancé she'd barely seen in two months and had come halfway round the world to be with.

The insulin bottles were still cold from the fridge as she rolled them gently between her hands to mix the contents. It was uncomfortable to inject cold insulin. Had John forgotten that bottles in current use didn't have to be refrigerated as long as they didn't get too warm?

Then she saw that these were new bottles and wondered if he'd just grabbed them quickly, having forgotten to get them out in advance to warm up. He saw her looking at them and confirmed that her guess was on the right track.

'They're Maya's,' he said. 'Had to borrow some. Left mine at home. She has a flat here. Maybe you didn't know.'

'Yes, she mentioned it, actually,' Summer answered, disturbed to find that his forgetfulness was worse than she'd thought if Maya was having to lend him insulin from her supply. Still, he'd already made it clear that he didn't want any lectures today.

She studied the labels and found that both were the newer human insulin she'd talked to Maya about only this afternoon, the same type that John used. Dr Macleay must have convinced her to make the switch, and she'd picked some up in town and put it straight in the fridge when she arrived home.

One bottle had the cloudy appearance of the slower-acting insulin, and the other was the clear 'regular' kind. The technique for mixing them together required precision and some patience but soon became familiar. The technique for injecting. . . Well, it was never 'as easy as brushing your teeth', as some medical people had been known to claim.

John was currently injecting a mixed dose twice a day, but Summer suspected that Dr Berg would try to persuade him to adopt a more complicated split-and-mix schedule that could have him injecting up to four or five times a day to achieve better control. She doubted this would happen without a fight, however, and was still groping for her own role.

Should I be making this easy for him? Or forcing him to tackle it himself?

She didn't know, and found that her voice was testy as she asked him, 'Now, do you have *any* idea which site you're up to?'

'No, I don't, and you sound like a nurse,' he growled.

'Well, you're asking me to act like one for you!' she retorted.

Then they both looked miserably at each other and reached for a rough embrace.

He made me believe in romance after my parents' divorce, she remembered. And he's only had this disease for four months. I can't expect us to get the balance right at once.

'Sorry,' he was saying, 'sorry, sorry, *sorry*!'

'It's OK, John.' She eased herself from his arms and felt her stomach drop at the sight of his handsome, brooding face.

Drawing up the clear insulin and then the cloudy, she flicked the barrel of the syringe to remove an air bubble, then said, 'How about your abdomen? We're a little late with this dose now, and it should be absorbed more quickly there than it would in your thighs or backside.'

'Fine. My thighs is where I've been using a fair bit.' He lifted his grey shirt—he'd changed since she'd seen him at five-fifteen, and looked very suave in a grey suit—and she pinched up a roll of smooth, olive-toned skin to the left of his navel, swabbed it, removed the needle cover, jabbed the needle in at a forty-five degree angle and heard him swear under his breath. 'I hate this,' he muttered through clenched teeth.

'I know.' She felt as guilty and pained as she always felt when injecting a small child who didn't understand.

Quickly she pushed the plunger, placed the swab over the end of the needle and withdrew it, pressing the swab over the spot for two seconds without rubbing. He was still wincing and muttering as she covered the needle again and snapped it off the syringe, then put both syringe and needle carefully in her garbage.

'Let's go, shall we?' she said, picking up her bag and putting on a smile.

'Sure.' He gave a reluctant grin. 'Guess I'm committed to eating now, whether I'm hungry or not!'

'Well, *I* am!' She was determined to keep this upbeat. 'I'm starving, and I've been in this gorgeous place for over two days, without tasting its seafood!'

He had his car outside, and as soon as they set off Summer lifted her face to let the mild breeze caress her tension away. . .which meant that she had several long seconds in which to be aware of Alex Page, standing at the hotel entrance in her powder-blue suit and lifting her gaze from the important new guests she was greeting to stare with real misery and longing at John.

Engaged in turning down the drive that led to the street, John himself was too intent on watching the road to have seen the other woman.

She really loves him, Summer acknowledged. It's not just spite or possessiveness that she feels. She loves him and I've stolen him from her, although I didn't know it.

It wasn't a realisation designed to enhance their evening together.

CHAPTER THREE

THURSDAY afternoons were quiet at the diabetes care centre. Neither of the two doctors had appointments until a late-afternoon session which ran from five until seven. Steve took time off, while Randall conducted an outpatient clinic at the hospital to treat other endocrine disorders such as hypothyroidism, dysfunction of the adrenal gland and endocrine-based infertility.

Ruth Garrick, the centre's part-time dietician, often used the time to conduct cooking demonstrations and nutrition counselling but today, instead, she and Summer were discussing the series of classes on diabetes that would commence next week.

Summer had taken some time off as well, leaving the centre at noon to shop in Hamilton before her meeting with Ruth at four. Shopping ought to have been fun, but somehow it wasn't. She'd bought presents for her parents—*separate* presents, of course—and then realised that she didn't even have an address for her father who was wandering the hippy trail in South-East Asia somewhere. And her mother's address was just that—an address. She hadn't seen the chic little London pad yet.

If John had been able to meet her for lunch, as she had suggested, it might have been nice. But he had pleaded pressure of work and it was true that Wave Crest Rose Beach was fully booked at the moment, mainly with tourists from the United States, and the resort's head chef was still threatening to decamp at a moment's notice, creating problems all round.

Their evening on Monday had been something of a

return to the mood of their courtship, with John filling it so full of eating, dancing and presents—a new swimsuit, pearls, flowers and an extravagant hat—that there had been little room for the serious discussion Summer had had in mind about plans.

Although, to be honest, couldn't she have pushed the issue if she'd wanted to? Instead, she'd told herself that they were taking some time to find each other again, and because he was a superb dancer there *had* been a reassuring harmony as they'd gyrated around the nightclub floor.

He had kissed her, of course, in the car outside her cottage afterwards, but it hadn't lasted long and he hadn't asked if he could come inside—which she had been expecting and had almost wanted. To deepen their physical intimacy might strengthen their bond.

Yes, she'd *almost* wanted it. Not quite, though, because—although he was so smoothly handsome that he could have graced the pages of a magazine as a model—her body didn't clamour with any urgent need to be joined to his. And it *should* be that way, shouldn't it?

The one man she had slept with in the past had similarly failed to arouse her very greatly. She had had a very foolish and very severe crush on Leon at the age of nineteen but had realised fairly quickly that that was all it had been and had ended it—to then see Leon find another woman within a week. This time there was more, and yet still the physical part was absent. Somehow she had retained her faith, though, that it was possible in the abstract and that it was possible for her.

It will happen, she told herself, and again, It takes time.

Which she and John didn't have if they never saw each other! Since Monday they'd had a drink before dinner yesterday and talked briefly on the phone twice, and tonight again, 'I'm working, late,' he'd said, 'But we'll have a great evening tomorrow.'

Working late. At least tonight I am, too!

She had offered to be here for the five to seven session after her meeting with Ruth, although Angela had been doubtful. 'Really? Your first week?'

'Honestly, Angela. Didn't you say you needed another fitting for your dress?'

So it was settled, and she was actually pleased at having plenty to do tonight.

Ruth Garrick was a nice woman, Summer quickly decided. In her fifties, she was a model example of what good nutrition and plenty of exercise could do, and she taught and practised yoga as well—which was, perhaps, what gave her smooth skin, glowing brown eyes and trim figure a softer, more relaxed aura.

After less than an hour they had agreed on who would conduct which part of the classes next week, and Summer felt confident that she'd perform her part well.

'I've taught a similar series a number of times before, of course,' she told Ruth. 'But here it's structured a little differently so I'll go over my notes now so that all goes according to plan.'

'I'll see you next week, then, if not before,' Ruth said as she prepared to leave.

It was ten to five. Lesley had just left too, with banking business to do in town, but the centre would soon be busy again. Anticipating Randall's need, Summer scooped decaffeinated coffee into the machine and set it going, then heard someone arriving outside. Not Randall nor Steve, and Imelda wouldn't be here as Summer was performing her duties as well as a nursing role tonight.

She went to look and found a very tense-looking couple who didn't manage to disguise the fact that they were sniping at each other, although they tried. He was very overweight while she was angular and thin, and it didn't take much effort to work out that he was the type two diabetic and she the concerned spouse.

'I still think you should mention it to Dr Macleay,' came an anxious, insistent whisper, not as discreet as the woman had intended it to be.

'Well, I'm not! All right? So give it a rest, Elaine!'

Becoming aware of Summer, hovering behind the reception window, they clammed up. He got out a magazine and plunged into it, ostentatiously ignoring his wife, while she sat on the edge of her seat—fidgeting and staring at him with a mixture of anger and concern.

'The doctors aren't in yet,' Summer said, 'but they should be any minute.'

There was a polite response, and Summer then turned her attention to her duties, running her eye down the appointment list and memorising the first few names so that she could get out their files. The sound of the two doctors' cars could be heard as she was still doing this, and the tense couple rose expectantly as they glimpsed Randall's entrance through the side door.

Summer said, 'I'll be taking a look at you first, Mr Davidson.'

She got out three more files then took the couple through to an examining room where she ran through some routine observations, including taking blood and a urine sample to test for protein, and got Mr Davidson himself to demonstrate the way he tested his blood sugar and read the result.

It was high, as had been most of the figures recorded in the diary he'd brought in.

'I told you,' Mrs Davidson said.

Her husband glared, and Summer came in quickly, 'Dr Macleay should be ready to see you now. He'll talk to you about the high readings and what you can do about them.'

'He knows—' Mrs Davidson began, then stopped

abruptly, frozen into silence by her husband's thunderous expression.

'Will you be going in too, Mrs Davidson?' Summer asked carefully.

'No, she won't!' came an angry growl just as Randall appeared, to say cheerfully,

'Come through, will you, Mr Davidson?'

He followed the doctor, clumsy on his feet, while Mrs Davidson attached herself to Summer, not realising that the latter needed to bring in Steve's first patient now.

'We've always had such a good marriage,' she said, clearly needing to talk. 'Better than most, I'd have said, for twenty-seven years, but this is destroying us, Nurse. He just won't accept that it needn't *be* serious if it's controlled. I have a diabetic friend who says she feels so much *better* now that she's been forced to lose weight and change her lifestyle, but if I so much as bring up her name. . . He just doesn't realise that I'm worried that if he goes on like this he'll *die* on me and I—I don't want to lose him! It's turning me into a nagging shrew!'

'Have you thought of going for counselling?' Summer said, hating to fob the woman off but aware that Steve and his patients were waiting.

Mrs Davidson was doubtful. 'We've always prided ourselves on solving our own problems. . .I know he'd be as devastated at the idea of divorce as I would.'

'Then make that your starting point,' Summer suggested. 'If you share that commitment to your marriage that's a very strong foundation.'

She knew it wasn't adequate advice but perhaps it would help a little, and after all her role was primarily to care for Mr Davidson's physical well-being. Emotionally, she could only point the couple in the direction of help.

Elaine Davidson's face had cleared markedly, though. 'Thanks. You're right. We'll keep trying.'

She looked much more at ease as she sat with a magazine, waiting for her husband's check-up to end, but when Mr Davidson emerged he looked angrier and more miserable than before.

'I'm *not* going to start injecting myself!' he muttered belligerently to his wife, and there was the sense of an impending explosion as they left the centre together.

After this the session went smoothly, with patients who should have been excellent antidotes for the less-than-happy atmosphere created by the Davidsons. One woman who had had gestational diabetes during pregnancy and had needed insulin to maintain her blood sugar within the normal range was now safely delivered of a healthy boy and her post-partum check-up today showed a complete return to normal pancreatic function.

Another woman was here to check her success with an insulin infusion pump, and that turned out to be going extremely well. She was thrilled with her level of control on the pump. 'I haven't had an insulin reaction or a bad meter reading since I started it. You bet I want to continue this way!'

Somehow, though, Summer's thoughts kept returning to the Davidsons, and when they entered the centre again just as she was starting to file away the patients' charts at the end of the evening she wasn't surprised. Steve had already left, and Randall. . .

'Can I see him again for a bit? I'm going to try the injections,' Mr Davidson said.

'I'm not sure, Mr Davidson,' Summer began.

But then Randall himself appeared behind her, swinging that mug of his, and said cheerfully, 'Come on in, Mr Davidson.' Summer took the mug from him finally, since he didn't appear to know what he wanted to do with it, and then returned to her filing.

She was just finishing ten minutes later when Randall

ushered the Davidsons through once again, and she heard Martin Davidson say to his wife, 'Thanks for sticking by me, sweetheart.'

'I know I've been a hag,' she sobbed, 'but to stand by and see you just walking into your grave. . .'

'It'll be better now. We'll read the books together, come to the classes next week and get it all down to a fine art. If you'd help me lose that weight too then maybe the insulin's only temporary and I can go back to the oral stuff. I was just so frightened you were going to leave me.'

'Oh, *never*, Martin!'

The door closed behind them and suddenly Summer was very close to tears herself. Why didn't Mum and Dad have that commitment? Her vision blurred and she bent her head over the last patient file.

'What, still here?' came Randall's cheerful voice, then, with an abrupt change of tone, he said, 'Hey. . . Hey. . .'

She straightened immediately and scrabbled for a tissue from the box at the corner of the desk. 'Sorry!'

'No, don't be.'

'Really, I'll be OK.'

She tried to pass him, her head down in a vain attempt to disguise her tears, but he reached out an arm and touched her neck with his fingers in a long stroke that painted her with warmth and effortlessly stopped her attempted flight with the gesture.

'Is it something I said?' he drawled softly.

The dry humour in his tone caught at her before she knew it and she gave a short laugh in spite of herself. 'You're really awful, aren't you?'

'I try to be. Got a reputation to keep up, you know.' He was still holding her lightly, just with one palm against the back of her head and the heel of his hand resting in the hollow of her neck. It meant that they were standing very close, and she was aware of his warmth and his scent.

'I've been awful for years, and everyone expects it now.' He sighed deeply. 'It's a burden, I can tell you.'

She laughed again. 'I'll forget why I was crying in a minute. . .or is that the idea?'

'You got it.'

'Isn't that wrong, though? People shouldn't bottle things up.'

'Laughing isn't bottling it up. And people also shouldn't unburden themselves to colleagues they've only known for four days. Would you thank me tomorrow if I wheedled all your love troubles out of you in a moment of weakness?'

'Not love troubles. Parent troubles,' she told him.

'Really?' He couldn't quite keep the surprise out of his tone and, not caring that she'd only known him for four days, she began to tell him about it—half expecting another teasing fob-off but not getting it this time.

Getting instead the very sober, focused regard of his blue eyes as he gently relaxed his caressing grip on her and lifted one hip to sit on the edge of the desk.

'. . .And the thing is,' she finished after a few minutes, 'they seem to be taking it all so lightly. They don't seem to hate each other or feel bitter.'

'Yes, I can see how that would be preferable,' he mused gravely. 'To have one's parents utterly miserable and at daggers drawn, incapable of being in the same room together.'

'*What?*' She was on the point of being angry, well aware of the slightly mocking tone and not seeing through it, at first, to what he was really saying. Then it struck her, 'You—you mean, *would* I prefer that? To have my parents hating each other? No, of course I wouldn't!'

She thought about it a little more and said with even more conviction, 'Of *course* I wouldn't! It just seems. . . such a waste, that's all, of all the work they've done. To me the commitment of a marriage and the growth and deepening of that bond year after year—like the Davidsons tonight, which is why I'm thinking about it, I suppose—is such a wonderful thing, and I feel they've thrown it away. I wonder if they really know what they're doing, out on their own, pursuing some dubious goal of independence and freedom.'

'Yes, it's always hard to see one's parents growing up and leaving the nest,' he said, far too seriously. 'It's natural to worry.'

'How can you keep making me laugh when I'm trying my best to *cry*!' she exclaimed, maddened.

He repented a little. 'I'm sorry, Summer. It just struck me that you really do share something with a mother whose chicks have left the nest. You're feeling lonely and abandoned, you're questioning some of their values and you're worried about them. Those are very natural and understandable reactions but, like a mother, you must recognise them for what they are—a mourning for something that inevitably had to pass.'

'Hmm. . .?'

'It's obvious to me, though, seeing you feel all this. . .' he slipped off the desk again and weighed a hand gently on her shoulder '. . .that they're very lucky to have a daughter like you, and should I ever meet them—and I must say I'm curious to meet two people who would name their daughter Summer Dusk—I would tell them so.'

'Well, thank you,' she said, then went on, because she was very distracted by his touch, 'And if you're wondering about Summer Dusk, they were hippies, of course—still are, actually—and that's when I was born. In summer. At dusk. In a cow-shed they'd converted to a cottage. They were very young at the time!'

'Like it, actually.'

'Thanks.'

She smiled up at him, aware of the heat and pressure of his hand still on her shoulder, and suddenly it wasn't safe any more—being alone here with him like this. Shadowed at the edge of her mind was the awareness that her body could respond to his with very little effort, and that must not happen.

He must have reached the same conclusion as his hand dropped to his side and he closed his eyes and rolled his shoulders, saying, 'Tense! Long day! I need to get home.'

'Sorry, I've kept you,' she answered, busying herself with her bag.

'It's OK, Summer.'

They locked up the centre together, saying very little—although she knew where he was at each moment and made very sure that she did not look at him or get close enough to touch. If he wondered how she was getting back to Rose Beach he didn't ask, just said a brief goodbye and went to his car, parked at the side of the building, while she crossed the road to the concrete shelter to wait for the bus.

It took a while to arrive, leaving her with plenty of time to realise that she felt better about her parents' divorce now than she would have imagined possible three months ago.

They didn't owe it to me to keep our family home just so I could come and stay on the odd weekend, she realised. Randall was right. I *am* reversing the roles a bit, playing the parent myself. They've made a choice that I don't think *I'd* have made, but it's not a tragedy—it's something to grieve over and then accept, and it doesn't have to change the way I live my life.

Except that if my parents hadn't been divorcing, I wouldn't have got engaged to John.

Where had *that* come from? It wasn't true, surely!

The bus arrived and she boarded it absently, grappling with the new notion and oblivious to the tropical beauty of her surroundings—vibrantly green and gold in the late light as a bank of bruise-purple cloud heaped in the sky to the west, slit through by shafts of sunlight.

Of course I'd still be engaged to him!

She tried to plot through the development of their relationship, the growth of their feelings, but couldn't disentangle her own emotions into clear strands. She had felt so adrift because of what was happening with her parents, and then John had anchored her again with his need for her. . .

She came within seconds of missing her stop and descended from the bus, still brooding over it all and no closer to an answer. Behind her, the limpid turquoise sea looked almost phosphorescent and she thought of walking on the beach to clear her head, but it was getting late and she hadn't eaten yet.

Not that I'm hungry. . .

The walk up the resort driveway felt good and then, as she reached the luxurious sprawl of the hotel building, she saw John's car parked at the front and knew that she had to see him. He wasn't in the office, though, where she had encountered him with Alex Page the other day so she left the building and then, knowing how claustrophobic her cottage would feel tonight, she took a roundabout route past the tennis courts.

At first, camouflaged herself by a row of oleander bushes, she didn't recognise the laughing couple who were coming towards her. It was Alex Page whose pale bell of blonde hair struck the first chord of recognition. And could that really be John beside her? He was animated yet relaxed as he regaled her with some lengthy, funny anecdote, and then was intent on her every word as she said something in reply.

There was no betrayal in their bodies—no illicit touch or kiss, no hint that they had recently made love. Nothing as damning or hurtful as that. And yet the truth was starkly obvious to Summer at once.

He loves her. Very much. So why on earth is he saying that he wants to marry *me*?

It was just then that they both saw her. Alex flushed, and her wide mouth tightened miserably.

John came forward to take her hands in his. 'Summer!' But his eagerness was forced, and the light in him had gone out.

Oddly enough, she didn't mind at all. It would have been harder if the thing had been more ambiguous. This way she knew at once what she had to do, and the fact that her own turmoil was ebbing by the minute told her that her own feelings had been as confused and misguided as John's.

It was the clearest insight she had had in weeks.

'I need to talk to you, John,' she told him.

'Hmm. . .'

He glanced uneasily at Alex, who lifted her head and said steadily, 'It's all right, John. We were finished anyway. I'll tell Maintenance that the surface of Court Three isn't safe, and I'll chew out the tennis pro for not switching courts or cancelling the session when he must have seen that there was a problem. Thanks for your help. Bye, Summer. Sorry I'm taking so much of his time this week.'

'That's all right.' Impulsively she reached out and touched the other woman briefly on the hand, but Alex flinched then tried to cover the reaction with a laugh that came out brittle and high.

She's trying so hard not to hate me, Summer realised, but she can't quite manage it and I don't blame her! This mess has to be sorted out!

Alex's heeled white sandals moved rapidly on the path as she disappeared into the thickening darkness. John was watching after her, frowning, and he took a pace forward as if to call her back.

'It's all right, John,' Summer said urgently. 'It's going to be all right. I promise.'

She reached for the ring that had never felt quite right on her hand and twisted it off, pinching her skin painfully for a moment, then pressed it into his palm and closed his fingers around it. 'Here. . .'

'*What*?'

'It's not right. It's a mistake. You must see that. Alex is in love with you and you're in love with her. And as for me. . . I—I've been using you, I think, without realising it, as a free ride away from all that was going on with my parents. But I'm coming to terms with all that now and—John, it would be a horrible mistake, you *must* realise that!' she finished heatedly, because he wasn't greeting her words with the relief she had expected.

In this light it was getting hard to see his features clearly, but that was quite a mess of emotions in his handsome face, wasn't it? Surprise, anger and . . .*panic*?

'You can't do this to me, Summer!'

'But, John, you don't love me. I *know* you don't!'

'Hell, OK, but I respect you. I care about you. How will I manage without you? How will I manage alone?'

'You're not seeing clearly. You won't *be* alone! Alex loves you, and after a decent interval—and probably not very long, at that—you'll be able to tell her your feelings and the two of you will be very happy.'

But he rejected this, turning away from her and pacing angrily. 'How could I do that to her?' he demanded, his voice harsh. 'How could I ask her to saddle herself with me when I'm a slave to meal plans and injections, and if I get it wrong I could be blind or legless in twenty years? I won't do it to her!'

Summer's spine tightened and chilled with shock, as if

she'd been doused in icy water, and her throat was so tight that for a minute she couldn't speak. She managed finally, 'Yet you're prepared to do it to me. . .'

'Because you're a nurse,' he told her, as if that should be obvious. 'You understand. You've seen it. You'd be going into it with your eyes open. With you there, the worst of it wouldn't happen, with any luck, and if it did you'd be able to help.'

'You mean *you'd* be able to fob off all responsibility for your control to me?'

He shrugged uncomfortably, not denying it. 'Makes sense, doesn't it, since you're already an expert?'

'So you were planning to marry me for the sake of my expertise.'

'Don't put it like that.'

'How *should* I put it, then?'

'It just. . .makes sense, doesn't it? I guess it's impossible now.'

'You're right there!'

'Look, I didn't mean to make you feel. . . Bloody hell! This thing hit me like a freight train four months ago and you were *there* from the beginning like an angel. I probably owe you my life. Without you I'd have holed up in a hotel room, gone on a sugar binge and just *ended* it with a massive bout of ketoacidosis. I wasn't using you. Or if I was it was as a rope to climb up out of hell. Aren't you strong enough for that? Do you really begrudge me that?'

He paced some more, then continued, 'I agree now. It's clear to both of us that it wouldn't work. I guess that's why I've been hiding behind work since you came, trying to find a connection with you again but not succeeding. But if you think that I'd ask Alex to take me back. . .' He laughed harshly. 'No way! *No way*!'

'Talk to Randall Macleay about it, John,' she begged him, finding a little forgiveness as her world shifted on its axis and a little of the professional entered her response to him once again. 'Talk to Randall about it, at least, before you close that door.'

And it was only much later, as she prepared for bed in her little resort cottage and played the difficult scene over in her mind again, that it occurred to her that she'd told him to talk to Randall, but Steve Berg was his doctor. Why had she make that mistake?

CHAPTER FOUR

SUMMER spent the whole of Friday at work, carefully hiding her bare left hand.

The breaking of her engagement, just four days after it had been made known to the other staff, was not something she wanted to announce just yet. And if there might have been a degree of professional difficulty in being engaged to one of the centre's patients, would it not be worse now that she was *not* engaged to him? It would all have to be faced soon, but if keeping her hand in her lap or curling her left thumb over the first joint of her ring finger could at least buy her the weekend. . .

I got this job so I could be with John, and now I'm *not* with John. Do I go back to England?

That was the most obvious and pressing question. It ought, perhaps, to have been an easy decision, but somehow it wasn't. With her parents both bound up in their new, separate lives she would have no obvious base from which to pursue job possibilities and a new living space. Land on her friends? She had them, of course—a small, loyal cluster—but changes were happening in their lives too. Liz was married with a new baby, Diana was about to embark on an exchange visit to Australia and Emily had moved back to her parents' be cosseted while she wrestled with her master's thesis.

I'm better off here, she quickly realised. A challenging job, a beautiful group of islands to explore. I'll stay. . . And yet I can't go on living in that luxurious resort cottage at the Giangrandes' expense.

That had been appropriate during her engagement,

although even then she'd been chafing for a permanent home. Now it was out of the question, despite John's somewhat harried assurance last night that she could stay as long as she wanted until her future plans were made.

No one at the centre seemed to be aware of Summer's circumspect behaviour with regard to her absent ring.

There was a bit of a buzz of secrecy in the air in any case, as it was Angela's last day and they were giving her a surprise send-off. She had been here for five years, predating everyone except Lesley Harper—since even Randall had only taken up his position as Director four years ago, after completing his specialist training in the United States and working in a hospital there for two years.

Under the pretext that Summer needed a last opportunity to learn the ropes, Lesley had persuaded Angela to come in straight after lunch, and Imelda was getting distinctly giggly as the time approached and the staff who had been invited down from the main hospital began to gather.

Randall seemed preoccupied, too, although surely it wasn't the impending party that was causing that frown and that dry, irritating whistling between his very straight white teeth.

'What *is* it, Randall?' Summer asked him crossly in the kitchen, where she'd discovered him idly in search of his blue mug and in the act of sneaking a curl of coconut from the top of Angela's cake just minutes before the guest of honour was due to arrive.

It wasn't, perhaps, the way she should have been addressing her superior at the end of her first week on the job, but he was evidently too wrapped in more important concerns to notice.

'What? Oh, this?' He whistled that dirge-like tune again. 'I'm just annoyed with myself, I suppose.'

'You're not the only one!'

'You mean because of the whistling? Sorry!' He

stopped, found his mug, poured coffee and then was whistling again by the time he left the room, without having explained just which personal foible was annoying him so much today.

The party went off well. Angela was splendidly, gushingly surprised, loved her appropriately large wedding present of two cane patio chairs and was in floods, suddenly, at the thought of leaving.

'It's the hormones,' she sobbed. 'I cried at a fast-food restaurant commercial on television last night. And it wouldn't have made sense to stay when Graham needs help with his business, and I'll be wanting to stay home with the baby anyway.'

She soon recovered, however, and ten minutes later Summer rather wished she hadn't as, being particularly preoccupied with the subject of rings herself at the moment, Angela suddenly noticed Summer's hand and said, 'Where is it? Did it get in the way at work, or—? Oh Summer, no!'

It was done, Summer thought with relief as she quite deliberately headed off to the botanical gardens to hide during lunch the following Monday. A few minutes ago, she had quietly told the gathered group of centre staff that her engagement was off, and had assured them that it wouldn't affect her commitment towards the new job.

'I told Angela on Friday, and I'll probably be taking over her flat,' she had explained.

'Yes, she was disappointed, initially, at the fact that you'd have no need for it as she was counting on handing it on to her successor,' Lesley had said, to cover the slightly uncomfortable moment when they'd all digested the news. 'Which explains why she hasn't given notice or arranged a sublet already. With everything else she's had to organise lately, she hadn't got around to doing anything about it.'

'Well, I'm supposed to be picking up the key from the landlady and taking a look at it after work tonight,' Summer had said.

Which arrangement had meant that this lunch break was her only chance for some time alone.

She felt good. A little buffeted by the fickle winds of fate, perhaps, but with the beginning of a more solid foundation than she had had for months. She was teaching this afternoon, and was looking forward to that. Two classes were scheduled. The first, which began at two, was part of an introductory series of five classes for newly diagnosed type one and type two diabetics and their families. The second, at half past three, was a one-off session for a smaller group, designed to answer more difficult questions and demonstrate some of the latest options in self-care such as jet injectors, electronic blood-sugar meters and insulin pumps.

It was a heavy schedule and went well, but ran late so that the centre seemed very quiet once the class participants had all left. In fact, after letting everyone out of the meeting-room through a side door and re-entering the open-plan office, Summer at first thought that she was entirely alone. Lesley's desk was tidied for the day, and she could see clean coffee-cups draining on the stainless-steel sink in the kitchen.

'Have they left me to lock up alone? Let's hope I remember the routine!' she murmured aloud, then was startled by the click of a door behind her.

Randall's door. He came out of his office, with his blue mug dangling from his index finger by its sturdy handle as usual, and wandered across to the sink to rinse it out. Summer looked at her watch. A quarter to six.

He must have caught the gesture from the corner of his eye, although after his first slight smile it hadn't seemed that he was looking at her at all. They hadn't seen each other during the afternoon and he'd stayed very much in the background of the small discussion about her broken engagement, and now she felt a sudden and very unnecessary urge to explain to him in more detail. She resisted it, fortunately. Beyond the bare fact of it, it was really nothing to do with him.

'Yes,' he said now, 'everyone else has gone. I had some things to catch up on so I said I'd wait for you and lock up.'

'And teach me how to do it properly, please, because I don't think I know the whole routine.'

'We shouldn't schedule those classes one on top of the other,' he pronounced. 'They do tend to run late. And,' he added, after a sharp glance in her direction, 'it's tired you out. We'll space them differently next time.'

'I'm fine,' she told him, although he was right. She *was* tired. But that was probably more to do with the strain of the past few days. 'I didn't want to short-change anyone, and they all had questions.'

'How are you getting home?'

'Oh, I'll just—'

She stopped abruptly, remembering that she had to change out of her uniform, walk half a mile to Angela's landlady's house to pick up a key, then catch a bus back to the flat and return to the landlady's on the way home to pay a deposit if she decided to take it. A little daunting, with over three hours of animated teaching still making her face muscles ache and her mind buzz.

And just at that moment rain spilled onto the ground all around the building with the suddenness of machine-gun fire so that the gutters, which collected the water and fed it into underground tanks, were soon running full. She groaned at the white curtain of water beyond the windows.

'Haven't you invested in an umbrella yet?' Randall queried easily, a grin thrusting his strong jaw forward a little.

'Not yet. And I don't think I'll bother now. Clearly I'd need to upgrade to a sealed plastic bubble to deal with this!'

'People do say, actually, that it rains a lot in England.'

'Nothing like this!'

'But it's better this way, don't you think?' he suggested earnestly. 'Buckets down for an hour, then it clears. Far more efficient. It'd take days for this lot to fall in England, wouldn't it? Like squeezing droplets from a damp sponge.'

'Efficient,' she echoed drily. 'I'll remember that, and I'm sure the fact that this rain is so *efficient* will keep me much drier!'

'Don't worry, I'll give you a lift,' he answered patiently. 'And before you start to argue—'

'Save your breath,' she told him, 'because I wasn't planning to argue at all! If you could drop me at the place where I'm to collect the key to Angela's old flat that would be great. I can manage the rest.' She outlined the arrangement to him briefly, then disappeared into the bathroom to put on a cotton print dress.

It was, as Angela had explained, just a short distance to her landlady's house in Randall's bright blue car. Summer hopped out and said a firm goodbye, unwilling to have him wait. But when she ran up to the house and knocked on the door—as loudly as she could above the pounding rain—there was no answer.

Perhaps it *was* the rain. No one could hear her above the noise. But, after prowling around as much as she dared, Summer had to admit defeat. There was some mix-up about the timing of her visit. . .or Angela's bridal jitters had made her forget to arrange it in the first place. No one was home.

'And what on earth I'm to do now, I don't know!' Summer said aloud as she subsided against the window on which she had been knocking. 'Go back to Rose Beach, I suppose.'

'No luck?'

She jumped at Randall's voice behind her. 'I thought you would have driven off!' Then she immediately felt an unabashedly selfish pleasure at seeing him there, representing a dry ride in a car instead of a wet wait at a bus-stop.

A renewed spurt of even heavier rain had half drenched him during the short walk up the path and steps from his car, which was hidden from sight behind jungle foliage below. The white shirt he wore was transparent in patches now, revealing the contours of strong shoulder muscles and the pattern of hair shading the wall of his chest—hair which was clearly even darker than the dark sable-brown on his head.

And if his shirt was transparent. . .she was suddenly aware of the way her own cotton dress clung to her rather slight but still very female curves. Automatically she folded her arms across her waist but that was worse as it brought her breasts together to create a small valley which glistened, at the moment, with the water that was dripping from her hair.

'Uh, no, I didn't drive off,' he was saying, not looking at her at all—very definitely not looking at her, although his voice seemed somewhat husky. 'Angela has been in such a dither lately, and I thought the plan about the key sounded a bit too complicated. Why don't we try the flat itself? Perhaps the woman is there?'

'I can't ask you to run me around like that.'

'Why not?'

'Because. . .I just can't,' she answered lamely.

'Don't, then,' he suggested, smiling crookedly at her now. 'I'll just whisk you off in my masterful way and leave you no choice in the matter. Aren't you anxious to get settled into this place?'

'Yes,' she admitted flatly, turning to look at the rain thudding on the glossy leaves beyond the veranda. 'I hate. . .where I am now.'

'One of the most luxurious resorts in Bermuda? Gosh, you *are* finicky!'

'Why do you do this?' she demanded, rounding on him and wishing that her height allowed at least the *possibility* of intimidating him. Since he stood a good foot taller than she was, though, it didn't.

'Do what?' he queried innocently.

'Cut straight through all the polite, *necessary* little fictions and insist on baring the truth.'

'Because I'm "awful". I thought we'd already agreed on that.' He seemed utterly unrepentant, and she *hated* his grin!

So, after a spluttering moment, 'Yes, well. . .' was her dark answer. 'I now see that "awful" wasn't nearly strong enough!'

And yet she wasn't really angry with him. There was something oddly comfortable about the apparently brutal way that he kept letting her know that he understood. He'd seen at once that her ring didn't feel right on her hand. Now he understood that she didn't want to be beholden to John. And, in the midst of it all, he actually managed to make her laugh!

'This is the address,' she told him as they regained the car and immediately began to fog up its windows with their mutual dampness.

He glanced briefly at the slip of paper she showed him. 'Oh, sure. . .'

'Oh, you've been there, of course, visiting Angela.'

'No, I haven't, actually, but I was born in Bermuda and it's not a big place.'

They reached the right address ten minutes later and she braved the rain again, after insisting that he wait in the car—under these conditions, her dress was only going to cling tighter the wetter it got—but no one was there and the place was uncompromisingly locked. The other three flats in the small block looked unoccupied at the moment too.

'Just drop me at the bus-stop,' she said to Randall, drenched and defeated, 'and I'll try to phone Angela later.'

'Phone her from my place,' he suggested casually.

'From your place?'

'Yes. I can't help myself. I'm a compassionate man beneath it all, Summer, and the thought of dropping you at a bus-stop when you look like a drowned—'

'Thanks!'

'Although, of course, a very *attractive* rat. . . No! It's really impossible. You'll have to come home and have dinner with me.'

She probably should have argued, but she didn't. His refusal to dissemble cut both ways and, frankly, the idea of companionship—someone else's genuine *home* instead of a resort cottage—and a meal that was neither five-star restaurant nor emptied out of a can into a small saucepan on the cottage's stove, which were her other two choices at the moment. . . She wanted it!

The rain had begun to clear now, as suddenly as it had begun, and the sun was setting. As they came back through Paget and past the hospital Summer could already see the clouds tearing themselves into tufted pieces overhead to reveal a darkening satin sky painted with glowing colours.

Along Front Street traffic was slow as tourists from the two huge and festively lit cruise ships at anchor there returned to their cabins after shopping expeditions or ventured forth again, having exchanged the day's casual beach-wear for more dressy attire. If those clouds continued to break up then it would be a gorgeous evening—mild, velvety and clear.

Neither of them said much until they were clear of the town, but their silence was relaxing after an afternoon of teaching and talking and then that wild goose chase over the flat. Randall had turned on the car's heater to dry their clothes, and the warm wash of air on her rain-chilled legs was like a phantom caress.

She loved the houses here! Every one of them was unique, it seemed, piled onto some odd elevation or set against the grandeur of a tropical garden, and all painted in pastels that would have looked garish in a colder and less sun-drenched climate. He had turned off the main road now, and was winding along within clear sight of the ocean. She saw a sign reading SPANISH POINT, a wonderfully sea-flavoured name, somehow, and now the houses she glimpsed all looked out to the blue horizon, as if watching for ships.

'Is this your place?' she asked, stirring herself quite reluctantly as he pulled into a tiny wedge-shaped parking place perched at the top of a short ramp just yards from the narrow street.

The cream-painted stone glared briefly in the headlights of the car before he switched them off.

'My parents',' he told her. 'They've gone sailing in the Caribbean so I'm running the place.'

'Nice! For how long? A week?'

He laughed. 'Try a year!'

'A year? They really *have* gone sailing! Don't tell me. . . Next they plan to go round Cape Horn.'

'Probably.' He grinned again. 'They've always been adventurous, and now that Dad's retired I wouldn't be surprised if they never really settled back here again. They've more or less said that the house is mine now. My elder sister lives in the Bahamas. Next they'll probably sail across and pay an extended visit to her. They love that boat.'

'And do you take after them? Oh!' She had caught sight of the name of the house on a small brass plate by the door, and no longer cared about an answer to her deliberately arch question. 'Lookingview. Has it always been called that?'

'Well, only since my great-grandmother's time.'

'Oh, "only" that long,' she laughed. 'It really is a family house, then?'

'Yes, for five generations.' He opened the door and ushered her in and, glancing back at him, she saw the pride and love in his face.

My goodness, he adores this place! she realised.

And she could see why. It wasn't large, although she suspected that the original dwelling had been even smaller. The additions, though, blended so well that she could only guess at the original layout. Huge windows overlooked a higgledly-piggledy garden, sloping down to the water of a sheltered bay, there was a tray-ceiling in this living-room and a beamed ceiling in the dining-room beyond, as well as two huge, thick-walled fireplaces.

At the windows there were slatted wooden blinds, or 'jalousies', that were pulled out at the bottom to open the house to air and light, and the Bermuda cedar in all sorts of places completed the typical Bermudian feel to the architecture. She could see the family's long associations with the place reflected in the odd yet delightful collection of household objects. An old butter-churn, a Victorian rosewood sewing table, a brass-bound barrel. . .all lovingly preserved.

With the feeling that she could study this place for hours and still not have enjoyed all its detail, Summer exclaimed, 'Randall, it's gorgeous!'

And he actually flushed, ran his hand along the time-polished surface of an old mahogany sea-chest set beneath the windows and muttered, 'Well, *I* think so,' and she could see that he was embarrassed at the degree of feeling aroused within himself. Embarrassed, too, at the fact that she had seen it, which was a side to the man that she hadn't observed before.

'You keep it very nicely, too, considering your mum's not here,' she teased, wondering suddenly about the ancestry that had given him dark hair and sooty lashes along with fair skin and sailor-blue eyes. Irish, perhaps?

'Ah, as to that. . . Someone comes in twice a week,' he admitted, and was at ease again.

Still curious about the details of the house, she began, 'I loved that set of steps to the front door that starts off wide and ends up narrow. . .'

'It's called a "welcoming-arms" staircase.'

'And what is that statue. . .is it a statue, or a very still ghost? The one that I can see in the garden. It looks like a woman's face.'

'Well, we don't have a ghost, *as far as I know*,' he answered seriously, then added with a wistful note, 'Although they do have one over at Tamarisk Hall in Paget, they say. A woman whose skirts can be heard to swish from time to time.'

'Friendly?'

'Yes, friendly, damn her!'

'You're jealous, aren't you?'

'Of course! I've always wanted a friendly ghost, and I can't forgive my ancestors for failing to oblige. Our mystery woman in the garden is only a ship's figurehead. I'll take you down and introduce you to her later, if you like. The garden is lit, see. . .' He strode to a wall-switch and flicked it to reveal a scene beyond the slatted jalousies that was almost like a stage set, with the setting sun behind.

The yellow glow of artfully placed floodlights brought

out a dozen different tropical greens in the lush foliage of palmettos, pawpaws, banana trees and olivewoods, as well as the blooming colours of Easter lilies, morning glory, poinsettia and bougainvillea, some of which were closed up for the night. The lighting did not reach as far as the water of the bay so the sea formed only a darkening backdrop to the eye, as well as a softly sighing background of sound.

'The garden's not large. It doesn't go beyond the water-tank, there to the left, but it blends well with the house, I think. Come through here and I'll show you. . . Or are you chilly in that damp dress?' His gaze took in the cotton fabric briefly but did not linger.

'No, it's almost dry now, after the heating in the car.'

He seemed to have forgotten his reserve, and she followed him through the dining-room and out to a garden room that could be opened to the air or closed off against a storm.

Altogether, their tour of living spaces, kitchen, four bedrooms and garden took nearly an hour, but Summer wasn't bored for a minute.

'But what are these houses made of?' she asked at last as they stood by the cool mass of the old above-ground water storage tank. 'Surely it's not cement?'

'No! Local stone. Coral-limestone. It's quite soft and creamy-coloured when it's first cut, and gets harder and stronger when it's exposed. Turns a sort of pale cloud-grey. Mostly painted, of course. Cut very thick and stays wonderfully cool. At this time of year, of course—' He broke off. 'Speaking of time. . .' He looked at his watch. 'Hell, it's after eight already, and I promised you dinner! My God, how long have I been boring you with all this? You must be starving!'

'No, not at all,' she told him. 'Well, yes, I'm getting hungry, but bored? No!'

'Well brought up, aren't you?' he grinned ruefully.

'No, I'm serious, Randall. Please finish telling me about—'

But he cut her off with a wave of his hand. 'It'll have to be salad and spaghetti with a quick tomato and onion sauce, I'm afraid. If I put the water on straight away then we can have a drink and some cheese and crackers while we wait.'

He set off up the stone steps and back into the house and Summer could only follow, although he categorically refused her offer of help in the kitchen. Behind them the cool garden was again in darkness.

'Sit down,' he ordered. 'Gin and tonic? Wine? Or something lighter?'

'Gin and tonic,' she said. 'But, really, I can help make the sal—'

'No!' His strong hands came to take her shoulders and turn her firmly into the living-room. 'Sit down!' he repeated, and just in case she was going to try and disobey the hands stayed where they were and caressed her firmly downwards into the comfort of a pale green couch.

Summer found the gesture oddly hypnotic, and felt as if she were moving in slow motion. His hands left her and he returned to the kitchen but for long seconds afterwards she could still feel the imprint of their warmth, as if they had been pressing her bare skin instead of the still slightly damp cotton print dress. It felt as if she had been wrapped in some warm fur stole, and she wished that it *was* something as tangible as that so that she could pull the feeling more closely around her.

This is the first time I've been in a real home since Mum and Dad put our place up for sale, she thought. And that was months ago.

Her room at the nurses' home attached to her London hospital, John's hotel room at Wave Crest Mayfair, the cottage at Rose Beach. . . None of those places were really a home.

Listening to Randall's efficient movements in the kitchen and letting her gaze wander over the quirky beauty of this room, Summer felt a sudden restlessness and disobeyed his order to stay where she was.

'Don't banish me to another room,' she told him, standing in the kitchen doorway. 'Can't I sit in here so we can talk? I promise I won't lift a finger to help you!'

'Well, I don't much like an audience when I cook,' he growled.

He had a simple sauce simmering on the range and had heaped pasta into a pot of boiling water. Now he turned to wash lettuce under a stream of water from the brass taps, the movements of his large hands deft yet casual.

'How about if I promise just to stare moodily into my drink?' she offered.

'That'll do.'

But she cheated. It was quite unconscious at first. Gin and tonic just wasn't a very interesting drink to stare into once you'd got past ice melting and bubbles breaking. Randall, on the other hand. . . The human eye was naturally drawn to a moving object.

Instinctively she noted the strong stance of his legs, set slightly apart as he stood at the sink, the square breadth of his hips, the wider reach of his shoulders and the gentle, reined-in strength in those hands as he broke the fragile lettuce and arranged it in a ceramic bowl. She had not been fully aware until now of the sheer physical power of his frame. It was not what one expected of a doctor, not what had made the strongest impression on her so far.

No, he moved with more grace than such a powerful man usually did and he spoke more thoughtfully, listened more sympathetically. This sensitivity was reflected in his face, too. The mobile lips, the blue eyes that could be far warmer than the colour blue had any right to be. . .

'You're not watching that drink!'

'Sorry. I'm not used to sitting round in idleness while someone else does the work.'

'Yes, you've given that impression in the office.'

'Have I?'

'I've rarely seen collating and stapling performed with such zest, for example.'

'I get bored, you see, and I fidget and. . .bite my nails.'

He laughed.

'Don't! It's a terrible habit, and I'm pretty sure I'm cured, but—'

'If you have a relapse tonight it will be my fault because I didn't give you enough to do?'

'Quite possibly, yes, so if there's any silver that needs polishing. . .'

He sighed. 'Here. Mix a vinaigrette, any way you like it. Will that keep you happy?'

'Thanks, Randall.' She took the vinegar and oil, mustard, salt and pepper and had an enjoyable time, sloshing them into a small glass jug and stirring until it looked about right, then realised that *he* had begun to watch *her*, which didn't seem fair!

She gave him a quizzical look and he acknowledged it wryly. 'OK. Just curious about you, that's all. How long were you planning to work after you married John, for example?' He clearly regretted the question at once, and said quickly, 'Sorry, if it's a sensitive topic. . .'

'Not really,' she replied cautiously. 'As I said this morning, our decision to end the engagement was. . .quite mutual.'

'Yes, I remembered that or I wouldn't have dreamed of bringing it up, despite my well-known frankness. We'll make it fair trade, if you like, and I'll tell you that I'm the victim of a youthful divorce.'

'Youthful marriage, don't you mean?'

'No, the marriage was positively *infantile*, I'm afraid.'

'Oh, dear!'

'Usual thing,' he explained, with a wry sort of cheerfulness. 'Both of us overworked med students, grabbing desperately for the illusory sanity of a relationship. The divorce represented quite a leap in maturity on both sides. It was made final a few months before I came back here from Boston. Final on paper, I mean. Emotionally, I'm only just over what it did to my faith in my judgement. So there, have I bartered my right to pry now?'

'Yes, although I think I might have got a good bargain. As for my working... John and I hadn't got as far as making plans for the future. All I knew was that I didn't want to be the kind of rich man's wife who spends her mornings shopping, has a long gourmet-and-gossip lunch, then tans in the afternoon, with a few work-outs and facials thrown in on the side.'

'So why did you—? No, sorry, I really can't ask that, can I?' He frowned, then laughed shortly. 'You definitely bring out the worst in me, for some reason.'

'If you were going to ask me why John and I got engaged in the first place...'

'Well, I was, but it was none of my bloody business, was it?'

'No,' she agreed gently, 'but I'd tell you if I really knew. We thought we needed each other, then discovered we didn't. That's as close as I can get.'

'Or as you want to get out loud.'

She rose to the light challenge. 'You were the one who reminded me, several days ago, that we've only just met.'

'So I did.' There was a short silence. 'I should learn to keep that sort of advice to myself, perhaps. It...uh... seems longer, doesn't it?'

'Yes,' she admitted, then added quickly, 'It often does

when you work with someone, I think. It's different from meeting socially.'

'Is it?'

They both looked at each other. Summer felt the quickening of her own breathing and an odd sense that time had slowed for a moment, stretching and distorting a little—like a music tape left on the sunny dashboard of a car. She was definitely feeling something. . .an awareness. . .and she didn't like it.

Not now, not tonight, clamoured her mind.

His lips parted on a controlled sigh of breath, then his nostrils flared and hardened briefly as he took in a long pull of air, giving him the look of a man who was winded but trying to conceal the fact. For what seemed like a very long time, they stared at each other in silence, and everything seemed very still and very expectant.

Then a moment later, 'Damn!' The explosive monosyllable punctuated the sudden violent hiss that came as the pot of spaghetti boiled over onto the stove, and Randall crossed to it in three strides to wrestle it away from the heat and into the colander resting in the sink. 'I forgot all about it. It'll be as soft as mush by now! And I haven't finished the salad or grated the cheese or heated those rolls yet!'

Now there was no more talk of her sitting down while he did the work. Summer grated the cheese, very glad to have something more to occupy her—her mind rather than her hands. Her awareness of him had been palpable and disturbing, the more so because she was fully conscious of the same heightened perception emanating from him. They were alone here and it was dark, and this sea-washed, time-worn cottage must have sheltered a dozen pairs of lovers, perhaps many more, during its long history.

The very walls and furnishings seemed to encourage sensual awareness. Summer wanted to run her fingers over the sheen of dark wood or green-gold brass, wanted to smell the pot-pourri set on a lace doily on the rosewood sewing table, wanted to listen for hours to the sea sounds drifting up from the bay and in at the open jalousies—and this hunger in her senses was too close to a different kind of hunger. To touch a man's skin, to smell its muskiness, to hear close to her ear the rhythm of breathing that was quickened by passion. . .

I shouldn't have come, she thought. But I mustn't think about *this*!

And what was this? *Nothing*! she insisted. Too much gin in that drink. Fatigue. The seductive effect of this old house. That was all.

'Hmm. Pasta's not as overcooked as I thought,' Randall said carefully a minute later. It seemed that he, too, had been looking for a safe way out.

And was he deliberately creating noise? The saucepan lid crashed back after he had tasted the sauce, the oven door clanged and squeaked as he put in the rolls to heat and bottles in the door of the fridge rattled as he reached in to put the cheese away.

'I might ring Angela,' Summer said when she had finished tossing the salad. 'It's after eight-thirty. Perhaps she'll be at Graham's and I can find out what happened and get the phone number to make the arrangement with Mrs Capshaw myself.'

'Phone's on the hall table.'

But there was no answer at the other end of the line.

'Let's eat,' said Randall when she returned to the kitchen.

They didn't use the dining-room but laid their plates on woven straw place mats at the kitchen table. Randall tossed blue linen napkins onto its polished wooden surface, as well as ceramic trivets to protect the table, then set the sauce down still in its pot from the stove. Everything else was laid out in a similarly casual fashion, including a bottle of rough red wine and two glasses which looked a little ominous to Summer. Hadn't the gin and tonic already done enough to blur the edges of this evening?

But as they ate and talked, a swimming glass of the stuff slipped down almost without her noticing. This was so nice. . . They talked about everything, it seemed. Work, politics, travel. Nothing *too* personal now, though. Nothing about relationships or the past. John wasn't mentioned. And, after they had eaten, it made sense to wash up together then move to the living-room with coffee and some wickedly dark liqueur chocolates he had found and studied sceptically. 'I hope they're not stale. . .'

They weren't.

'Are you falling asleep, Summer?' Randall said at last when she had lost all sense that perhaps she should not be here, should ring Angela again, should have got him to drive her back to Rose Beach hours ago or, better, ordered a taxi.

'Not falling asleep,' she murmured lazily. 'A bit dreamy, though. I was counting on the coffee to pep us up a bit, but somehow. . .'

He smiled ruefully. 'That's not surprising. It was decaf. Sorry. I should have offered you a choice.'

'No, it was lovely. But what's the time?'

'No idea,' he grinned. 'Does it matter?'

'Well, office hours, hospital visits and a class tomorrow. And I *must* get that flat fixed up. I think I should be—'

'Of course. You're right.' His manner changed abruptly and the lazy grin disappeared. 'Hang on. I'll check the clock in the dining-room.'

He uncurled long legs from where he had casually dangled them across the arm of the couch and padded in bare, tanned feet—she hadn't seen him take his shoes off—to the darkened doorway of the next room, returning a moment later to announce with a helpless expression, 'Actually, I hadn't realised it was *that* late—ten past eleven.'

Summer sprang to her feet. 'My goodness, it's far too late to ring Angela, which means I've lost another day.'

Would have to spend another day at Rose Beach, she meant, at the expense of her ex-fiancé's family.

Their eyes met and she knew that he was thinking, as she was, of John. Randall pulled car keys from his pocket and jiggled them. 'Let's get going, then.'

'No, I'll get a taxi.'

'And wait another half-hour for it to get here? You won't!'

'No, all right. If you don't mind.'

'Not at all.'

'I've left my bag somewhere.'

'Yes, I remember seeing it.'

'I'll just—'

'Now let's think—'

They spoke and moved at the same time, cannoning into each other clumsily. Summer received a sharp knock on her temple and Randall was clutching his jaw with one hand and her shoulder with the other, in order to steady them both. Summer saw stars and swayed.

'Oh, hell!' the doctor rasped.

'It's all right. . .'

'Are you sure?' Both hands had come around her now, warm and heavy, one cupping her hip while the other slid against her back, and suddenly neither of them was thinking of bumps on the head.

His arms tightened caressingly, pulling the whole length of her against his strength and warmth. He groaned.

Summer surrendered at once, her own strength draining away with frightening speed with the wine and their collision and the lateness of the hour. Their mouths found each other's effortlessly and their kiss was hungry, feverish, explosive.

And endless.

Randall muttered unintelligible words and she felt them only as fluting movements against her lips. Her hands splayed as she ran them down his back to explore the plaiting of sinew and muscle and then the hard contours of bone at his hips.

His maleness was flagrant and made her aware as never before of the fact that she was female, the counterpoint and complement to him in every way. Her flesh seemed to fit and mould against his as if they were two pieces of a puzzle, even clothed as they were. So this was how a true physical response felt. . .

Unbidden, the image came to her of how closely they might fit if there were no clothes between them.

'No!' The denial was as much a warning to herself as to him.

This was far, far too soon. Just three days ago she had been engaged to someone else, and though she knew now that she hadn't loved John she wasn't remotely ready to start exploring what she might or might not feel for Randall.

She pulled her mouth away from his and turned her head, which only made his lips travel in a fiery trail across her cheek and into the warm, tender hollow between her neck and her shoulders, sending threads of tingling heat through her with the speed of light.

'Summer?' he muttered, seizing the moment and nuzzling her collar-bone, then moving lower so that he almost reached the high, tender slopes of her breasts.

'It's too soon.'

This time, speaking the knowledge aloud, she was able to tear herself from him to stand just inches away, breathing heavily as his eyes held hers like powerful magnets.

'Of course.' The words caught for a moment in his throat, and she knew that her own words had been equally husky and lacking in control. 'Of course it is,' he added, his voice firmer now, but dark and still velvety with sensual need.

'You see, I—'

'Don't say anything, Summer. You don't need to. We've got quite a precedent for being frank with each other now, so you might as well know that I'm *aching* with disappointment, but I understand completely and you don't need to be afraid I'm going to push.'

'Push?' she echoed on a shaky laugh. 'A light tap in the middle of my back would do it, I think. There! That's frankness for you!'

'Appreciate it, actually...'

'Good! Because it's embarrassing and not easy!'

'...but all the same, no "light taps" either.'

'Thanks...'

He stepped away from her at last and forced his hands to his sides, then took the keys from his pocket once again. 'Um... Your bag.' Which was how this thing had started in the first place.

With a tremendous effort of memory and will she said, 'Oh... That's right. I left it behind the couch.' Hours ago.

He stood where he was while she retrieved it, and as she bent down for it, feeling her cheeks still flaming, she thought in bewilderment, What am I supposed to do with this physical pull? I know Randall is standing there in the hall and I could just drop this bag again and go to him even now...

'Ready?' His voice seemed to come from far away, distorted as if she were hearing it under water.

'Ready,' she said, aware of the deeper significance of the word and feeling very frightened by it.

She *wasn't* ready!

CHAPTER FIVE

'I WANT to learn how to test my blood glucose and start on multiple insulin shots, Sister Westholm,' said the bright young woman who had come in for an appointment at her own request one Monday morning.

'Well, we certainly encourage self-monitoring of blood glucose these days,' Summer answered. 'And then it makes sense to use the information to achieve better control by injecting more often. But is there a special reason for wanting to do it now? Have you been having insulin reactions or spilling sugar?'

She hadn't met Penny Malley before, but had given her advice over the phone a couple of times over the past few weeks, and knew from a reading of her file that twenty-one-year-old Penny had been an insulin-dependent diabetic since the age of four, and had been very rebellious and out of control in her late teens.

'Not more so than usual,' Penny answered. 'But "usual" means that I do occasionally have a reaction or get a high reading on my testing strips, and I've been reading about that ten-year study in the United States. You must know the one I mean.'

'The Diabetes Control and Complications Trial?'

'That's it. Sister Westholm, I *don't* want to go blind or lose my kidneys or my feet!'

'Of course you don't!'

'I don't care how much effort it takes, or how many times a day I have to prick my finger and stick a needle in my thigh!'

'Well, you're right, it *is* extra work and you'll need

some time with us to learn to handle it all properly.'

'It'll be worth it,' Penny insisted.

'Dr Macleay will want to see you for a good talk, then.'

'He's not here now? I was hoping we could get started straight away.'

'He should be here but he was on call at the hospital and he's been delayed.'

There had been an emergency admission earlier this morning, Summer knew—a man of twenty-four in a coma, which had quickly been diagnosed as acute diabetic ketoacidosis. Randall had made a quick call to the centre to explain, and she had happened to answer. He hadn't given much detail. In fact, he'd been quite abrupt, almost evasive, which was nagging a little at the back of her mind.

Now he was fighting to bring the man's blood sugar down, get his electrolyte balance under control and save his life. She didn't explain this to Penny. The young woman didn't need scary stories about other patients, having lived with fears about her own health for long enough.

'But why the urgency, Penny?' she asked with gentle curiosity. 'The results of the Boston D.C.C. Trial have been out since 1993, and I know Dr Macleay emphasises the direct link between good control and fewer complications to all his patients now.'

'Well, I've grown up, I suppose. I want to be realistic and take charge of my life now, and. . .' the pretty brunette flushed '. . .I've started going out with someone I like quite a lot.' This last phrase was clearly an understatement. Penny Malley was in love. 'And it wouldn't seem fair to him if I didn't do everything I could to keep myself in good health. Of course I. . .I haven't even told him yet that I'm diabetic.'

'Well, plenty of time for that,' Summer said cautiously. She had agonised over this question in the past with other patients. Exactly when was the right time for that sort of revelation?

'No, but I feel I should,' Penny said with a frown. 'I'm deceiving him this way, sneaking off to take my insulin injection before dinner and not letting on how carefully I control what I eat. He thinks I'm on a diet. He teases me about it because, of course, being overweight is one health problem I *don't* have!'

She gestured with pardonable smugness at her neat figure.

'Are you scared to tell him, Penny?' Summer asked.

'Yes, oh, *yes*! Of course I am!'

'I know. . . It's hard,' she murmured.

She had no advice to give, no reassurances. Every case, and every relationship, was different. Finally she said, 'You'll just have to trust yourself to know when the time is right. . .and trust him not to let it make a difference.'

'Yes. . .' Penny agreed miserably, then she brightened a little. 'And if I can tell him that I'm on this new system of self-monitoring, which will give me better prospects for long-term health. . .'

'Listen, Dr Berg is booked solid this morning, too, or I'd suggest you see him, but I'll see if Dr Macleay can fit you in for a longer appointment tomorrow, shall I?' Summer suggested. 'Then you and I will be able to get to work on learning the new techniques and scheduling.'

'I would like to get onto it as quickly as possible,' Penny said. 'And, when I'm comfortable with it all, then I'll tell Larry.'

'You might find that the right moment just happens along all by itself before that,' Summer suggested.

'Maybe. . .' Penny was clearly very nervous about the whole question.

When she had gone Summer wondered if there was more she could have said or done to help. But I don't know this Larry of hers, she thought. I have no idea how he'll react. No doubt Randall will have some ideas. He's always so tireless in going in to bat for his patients over these major life issues.

She couldn't help smiling a little as she thought this, remembering him on the attack recently over the issue of Alan Gregory's job as a waiter at the Ocean Charm restaurant. Randall had won that fight hands down after some very convincing threats about lawsuits and boycotts, which he'd been rather comically relieved about not having to carry through.

'Couldn't see myself spending my weekends marching up and down in front of the restaurant with a placard,' he'd said. 'I'd rather be sailing!'

'A placard? God, no!' Steve Berg had exclaimed in horror, his brow rumpled like a bad load of laundry.

'Did do it once or twice as a student,' Randall had reminisced, leaning back in a swivel chair in the middle of the open-plan office. 'Can't even remember what the issue was now. That's embarrassing, isn't it? Might it have been Save the Pigeons? No, *Spay* the Pigeons.'

'Randall, I never know when you're joking,' Steve complained.

'Neither do I, sometimes. . .'

Silly bloke!

Summer was still smiling. That nutty humour of his had been very useful. . .was *still* useful. . .in smoothing over any awkwardness between them following her dinner at his house. Whenever she felt any slow rising of heat within at an accidental touch or a shared look held for too long he would be certain to come up with something outrageous, and have her spilling over with laughter in seconds.

They both knew, though, that the heat hadn't really gone away. It was there in every exchange between them, no matter how casual—every chance meeting up at the hospital, every carefully professional consultation over a patient. . .

Randall returned from the hospital fifteen minutes later. He looked exhausted, and several strands of his dark hair were even darker with sweat as they curled against his temples and his strong, lean neck. He greeted Summer very briefly, not meeting her eye, and merely nodded at Lesley Harper who was on the phone. Dr Berg was in his office with a patient who had been on Randall's list, and the latter's next patient hadn't turned up yet.

Actually, it was Brian Page, the recalcitrant teenager whom Summer had encountered on her first day, and it would be predictable if he didn't keep his appointment at all and had to be chased down. On this occasion Summer was glad. Randall was clearly in need of a break. He had disappeared into the kitchen at the edge of the open-plan office and was heaping fresh coffee into the coffee-maker. China rattled on the metal draining-board of the sink, and a moment later he said to the room in general, 'Where's my mug, do you know?'

Summer, catching up on a paperwork before a scheduled class to be taught in tandem with Ruth Garrick on diet and food exchanges for type two diabetics, looked across at him and complained facetiously, 'You need to get yourself a duplicate. *Several* duplicates, better yet.'

He didn't reply, and only after some random opening and shutting of cupboard doors did there come a muttered, 'Here it is! In the cupboard. The new cleaner must have put it away again.'

'Put it away! In its right place! How illogical!' Summer teased, but for once there was no response. He just hung over the coffee-machine, watching the slow, steady brown drips begin to pool in the bottom of the glass jug.

'Sit down, Randall,' she suggested gently. 'It'll be a good ten minutes yet.'

'What? Oh, yes, I expect it will. . .'

'You had a rough morning?' she asked.

'Yes.' He sank into a black vinyl swivel chair, his long legs anchored to the floor while he twisted absently from side to side. 'We. . .nearly lost him, actually.'

He gave a sharp glance in her direction, as if assessing her somehow, and she took in a startled breath then felt her spine crawl. Something had happened. This was more than just fatigue and the aftermath of a close call.

'What happened?' she asked woodenly.

'His blood sugar was incredibly high when he came in,' Randall explained in a careful, neutral tone. 'Almost 2,000.'

'Wow!'

'I hadn't got there yet and the resident panicked and brought the level down too fast, so he went straight from that acute hyperglycaemia into insulin shock without regaining consciousness. In fact, he's. . .still not conscious.'

'Brain damage?' Summer asked with a frown.

'No. No, definitely not!' It was authoritative and yet. . . was he less sure than he seemed? She still didn't understand quite why he was giving her these details in such a careful way.

'I picked up the hypoglycaemia in time to avoid any chance of brain damage,' he was saying now. 'And we gave him fifty per cent glucose intravenously. The blood sugar was still slightly high from that when I left—about two hundred milligrams per decilitre, but it was better to bring it down gradually.'

'Oh, of course. . .'

'We can't afford another episode of insulin shock like that first one. Meanwhile, we were working to clear the serum and urine acetone and correct the dehydration and electrolyte imbalance. He should regain consciousness soon, and I think he's out of danger. . . But, Summer?'

'Yes?'

'The thing is. . .' He suddenly rose and took both her hands in his so that she stood instinctively as well, her heart pounding, and scarcely felt the caressing rhythm of the balls of his thumbs against her knuckles. 'It's John.'

'Oh, God, no!' She felt the strength drain from her legs and had to sit down again at once, pulling her hands away from his chafing touch to hold the edge of the desk tightly.

'I didn't know the best way to tell you. He *is* out of danger.'

'Yes. . . Thank you,' she answered vaguely, as if it was a special favour he'd done for her.

'You still care, don't you?' came the quiet question.

She answered it automatically, 'Of course I do!' Then she realised what he was asking and looked up, alarmed, to meet his searching, troubled gaze. 'Not—not like *that*, Randall.'

'No?' The small word contained a wealth of subtle references to their attraction to each other, its consummation as yet only hanging in the air as a shimmering, uncertain possibility.

'As a friend. And a patient. . . No, of course it's more complicated than that.' She felt, with some intuition she didn't question, his scepticism. 'Anyway. . .' She shook her head impatiently, not wanting to think of herself and Randall right now. 'The important thing is—how could it have happened?'

'I was hoping you might be able to tell me. . .'

'No! I haven't seen him. I moved into Angela's flat two days after. . .that dinner with you, and I've spoken to him once by phone to tell him my plans and that I was settled.'

'You've been avoiding each other.'

It was a statement, not a question, and she admitted edgily, 'I—I suppose we have, a bit. It's natural, I think.'

She looked up, a little defensively, and saw his slow nod. 'He came in to see Steve a couple of times that week about changing his insulin schedule but, as chance would have it, I was up at the hospital or in the middle of a class both times. I wasn't avoiding him then.'

'Still, that's four weeks ago now.'

'What's your point, Randall?'

'Just wishing there was someone with more of an insight, that's all.'

But she felt judged, slightly, until he ran a hand along her cheek and said, 'Sorry, Summer. Perhaps it's Steve I should be hounding about John's emotional state. He may have some clues. It's a pity I was the one on call.'

'No! I'm sure you've done everything—'

'Technically, medically, yes, but there's so much more to it than that with this disease. I wonder if Steve has assumed too much about his emotional adjustment.'

'He's certainly had the usual problems of anger and denial.'

'Which everyone expresses in a different way. Would you. . .be able to go and see him, Summer?' His look probed.

'Of course. I'll go after work tonight.'

'I. . .wasn't sure how hard this would be for you.'

'Well, it *is* hard, to be honest. . . But, as I said, I do care, and I want to go.'

Awareness hung in the air again, but there was no time to pursue it, or even to feel it for more than a second or two, as Lesley was approaching.

Randall said quickly, 'Anything happen at this end that I should know about?'

Summer told him about Penny Malley's visit and her desire to begin blood-glucose testing instead of the easier but far less accurate urine testing.

'Good for her!' was Randall's response. Lesley was

distracted for the moment by some papers on Imelda's desk. 'I was going to talk to her about it myself,' Randall went on, 'but I was waiting a few more months. It's only a year or so since she was playing chicken with fate by being as careless about control as she could. Now she's a model patient. It's a big transition, but if she's ready. . .'

'Well, I think there's an extra impetus come into the picture quite recently.' Summer told him about the new boyfriend, although she didn't say anything about the unmistakable glow in Penny's eyes and the corresponding fear that it would not work out.

'Hmm! He could be a lucky man!' was Randall's assessment. 'I hope he's good enough for her!'

Which was, Summer knew, his way of saying, I hope he doesn't lose interest once he finds out about her disease.

Lesley, arriving in time to overhear, gave her rather masculine laugh. 'You sound distinctly like a doting father, I'm afraid!'

'Yes, well. . .' he growled. 'Can't help that! It's the thing that really gets my blood up.'

Clearly, Lesley didn't quite know what he meant. Doting fathers got his blood up?

Summer understood. It was like his reaction to the issue of Alan Gregory's job at the restaurant. He just couldn't tolerate prejudice against his patients because of their disease.

'Brian Page's mother just called,' Lesley said. 'She got him up out of bed this morning for his appointment and thought he had left to come in, but she just found him in their den, watching videos. Apologised profusely.'

'He's old enough to keep his own appointments,' Randall said.

'I'll chase him up to make another one,' Summer offered, glad of the distraction.

* * *

John's eyes were closed, and he hadn't yet realised that anyone was there. Summer stood in the doorway of the private intensive care cubicle, her feet unable to move for a moment. Her heart was in her throat, which was tight and constricted, and hard tears were pricking in her eyes.

This was how she had first seen him in England—when they had each been drawn to the other by misunderstood needs. Now that time had passed she could see the man he really was much more clearly and her own need had gone, but that didn't mean that she felt nothing for him.

'John. . .' She spoke too softly and he didn't hear, although she didn't think he was asleep—just shutting out the harsh world for a while.

He looked terribly ill. Pale, and several pounds thinner than when she had last seen him four weeks ago. His lips were dry, as was the rest of his skin, and the blue patterned hospital gown, pulled crookedly across his chest, made him seem intensely vulnerable.

He stirred, his lids fluttered and opened and she stood frozen, watching him. At first he didn't even seem to recognise her, then he murmured, 'Summer?'

'Yes. Yes, it's me,' she said tremulously, crossing the small space and taking his brown hands in hers.

'Thanks,' he whispered.

'What *happened*, John?'

He didn't pretend not to understand, just shrugged weakly. 'I thought maybe if I stopped taking the insulin it might jog my pancreas into producing its own again. After all, it managed to for those few weeks just before you came over.'

'Oh, John. . .!'

'OK, crummy theory. But I can't *handle* taking those shots day after day after day. And Alex has been trying to make me let her help, and that's just—' He didn't bother to finish, just laughed.

'It sounds like you should take her up on the offer,' Summer suggested.

'Don't be an idiot!'

He lay in silence for a moment and she asked, 'Would you like me to leave?'

'Well, no point in your staying, really. Thanks for making the offer, but I'm still pretty shattered and—'

'It's all right, John. Just wanted you to know I was around.'

'That's good of you. Come again in a couple of days. They say I'll still be here. . .'

'I will. Has Alex been in?'

'No! And I won't have her told, OK? Mum and Dad wanted to, and I wouldn't let them. Alex thinks I'm in New York. So, if you go interfering—!'

'I won't,' she told him quickly, 'if you're sure that's what you want. But I can't help feeling—'

'Leave it, Summer. It's not going to happen for her and me, and I'm just going to have to accept that.'

'All right, John. . .'

He looked totally wiped out now and Kathy Lemmon, one of the nurses she knew by this time from her visits to other patients, was beginning to hover. 'I need to take his observations in a couple of minutes, Summer.'

'Of course.'

She left again, thinking, My relationship with him feels so long ago, so short, and so *impossible* now. We would have been so wrong for each other!

Randall was waiting for her when she returned to the centre to collect her things. Steve was still in his office, working on a paper, but Imelda, Lesley and Ruth had gone. Seeing him there, Summer steeled herself for questions but they didn't come, and when she realised that he wasn't going to probe about John she gave him a look of such relief that he smiled, bringing a sigh and a smile from her as well.

'Thanks, Randall. . .' she muttered vaguely, and he didn't seem to think it strange that she was thanking him when he hadn't even spoken.

'Like to come sailing?' he asked laconically.

'Sailing?'

'Yes.'

'*Now*?'

'Why not? The forecast is good.'

'Is it? Well, in that case, what other factors could there possibly be to take into consideration?' she drawled sarcastically.

'Exactly. You tell me. What other factors are there?'

'Um. . .'

'Good. We'll have dinner on the boat,' he announced, as if it was settled, and somehow it was.

The shadows were lengthening but the sky was still blue, and a fresh breeze created a uniquely marine kind of music as Summer stepped in rubber-soled sneakers onto the wooden walkway of the marina in Randall's wake an hour later—after he had taken her home to change and they'd stopped for some provisions.

Dozens of yachts were moored there, and their aluminium masts clinked and resonated as their nautical ropes bumped back and forth against them. It was a sound that seemed to conjure up instant images of adventure, and she thought of Randall's parents away in the Caribbean. He had brought a couple of their postcards into the office last week with the report, 'No sign that they want to come home!'

She had been in touch with her mother, too, over the past four weeks, and Flower Westholm had taken the news of her daughter's broken engagement with breezy unconcern. 'You're quite right to break if off, darling, if that's what your intuition is telling you. No doubt it all forms part of the cosmic plan.'

David Westholm was, apparently, uncontactable in Tibet. 'I really don't think he *wanted* any of us to know how to reach him for a while,' was Flower's explanation. And somehow their divorce didn't seem nearly as incongruous and impossible as it had done just a few weeks earlier.

Summer needed only a light jacket against the breeze, and its salty freshness took away the strains of the day. Beneath the jacket, she wore cream canvas jeans and a turquoise and white blouse in a nautical print, having chosen it because it was cool and fresh, and hoping now that Randall wouldn't think it silly to dress like a would-be sailor.

Not many people were planning to sail this evening, it seemed. Only a few of the boats had crews at work, preparing to take them out. Randall made a leap onto the wooden deck of a comparatively modest craft—a surprisingly agile and graceful movement for such a powerful man. 'Here she is. Not exactly in the millionaire class, but room to swing a kitten, if not a cat.'

Then he held out a hand for her to jump, too—by no means as gracefully, as the deck looked about forty feet below as she sprang towards it. The leap was even harder than it looked. The boat dipped under her weight and she nearly fell, but his strong body was there to shore her up, and the warmth and pressure of him made her gasp. Her face had almost cannoned into that hard chest.

'We'll practise,' he drawled.

'Thanks for the support!'

'Sorry. . .' He wasn't! 'Wait here while I change.'

He disappeared immediately below deck and emerged a few moments later, wearing cut-off jeans that had faded and frayed into a bleached fringe just at the very hardest part of his long, muscular thighs. A blue and white boat-necked T-shirt was flung onto his strong torso, and his ankles were bare and just slightly browned above old canvas sailing shoes. If she had been in any doubt before, the ensemble—and what it revealed beneath—told her how often he did this.

'Got a few things to do,' he said. 'Want to help?'

'Oh, he won't let me help him cook,' she told the aluminium mast, 'but this, which I know nothing about—as he reminded me himself only minutes ago—he wants help with!'

But he seemed to be restraining his more merciless impulses tonight and, apart from confusing her completely by calling the ropes 'sheets', he soon got her to feel quite at home and almost useful.

The boat was called *Aquamarine* and, like the name, it was a jewel—a little gem of a craft, with its white-painted deck and exterior, and glossy wooden cabin.

'Only eighteen feet. Four berths,' he explained in snatched phrases as he clambered about, those denim shorts tightening across his taut male behind whenever he stretched or bent. 'I bought it when I first got back from Boston. I'd been saving for it there, actually. Every time I stashed away some dollars in that special bank account it stopped me temporarily from feeling so homesick. But, then, once I was back here I had to ride a scooter around for the next six months until I could afford a car, which wasn't very seemly for a man in my position. Had my priorities a bit wonky, there. . .'

'I don't think so at all,' Summer told him with a grin. 'You could get to work on a scooter perfectly well, but I don't imagine the waters around Bermuda are very suitable for, say, canoes.'

He laughed. 'Good point. I like your perspective on the

matter! Hope you feel the same after you've got to know her more personally. You've never sailed before?'

'No, but I've always thought I'd like to try,' she answered. 'Which, I suppose, is what everyone says.'

'Pretty much,' he admitted. 'Some mean it more than others. . .and some you *hope* mean it more than others.' He grinned, and she felt her pulse quicken.

He had started a small auxiliary outboard motor, untied the ropes that had fastened the boat to the marina's wooden deck, and coiled them neatly on cleats. Now he was steering the small craft out of the cramped confines of the marina and into the calm water of the bay, before shutting down the engine and pulling the main sail aloft.

'I have a spinnaker for *Aquamarine*, too,' he told her, 'but we won't use that tonight. Spinnakers are for windy afternoons when you really want to feel the breeze raking through your hair.' He slid his fingers through the short dark strands as he spoke. 'Now, do you want to learn a bit about tacking?'

An hour later, they stopped to eat. Randall had spent twenty minutes giving her her first very basic lesson in sailing as they scudded in a zigzag line across the bay, and then he had poured her a lemon squash that clinked with ice and ordered her to sit back while he managed *Aquamarine* alone. She had watched him rather dreamily as he clambered about the boat, noticing how his shoulder muscles became taut as he wound winches or hauled on lines and enjoying the strong planes of his profile silhouetted against the early evening sky.

How did he know I needed this? she wondered. I didn't know I needed it, but I do, and he's making it so perfect. . .

They were out of the breeze now, and the big sail was quiet as Randall gently eased the boat into the shelter of an island where a handful of lucky Bermudians owned get-away cottages. Darkness had almost fallen. The sky was a dark blue that showed new stars every minute, and lights from the shore had begun to reach golden fingers across the blackened water. Randall lowered the sail and anchored the boat, and now the only sounds were those of water, lapping at the hull, and wind, singing a high song in the rigging and canvas above them.

'What are we eating?' Summer asked. 'And how can I help? I've never cooked in a galley before, but I'm quite willing to learn how.'

'No cooking necessary,' he told her. 'It can be fun, poking around down there in my tiny stove, but not today, and so everything is cold—and not even home-made.'

'Not home-made! Well, I'm getting off this boat at once!' Summer teased.

'If you do, you'll be insulting one of the oldest catering concerns in Bermuda,' he said. 'It's run by a friend of my mother's, Helen Burkett, and I wasn't very specific about what I wanted, since it was at extremely short notice. I just asked for a picnic, so we'll see what she's given us. Whatever it is, it's bound to be good. . .'

He went below and brought up the two cartons he'd stowed when they'd boarded, and took from them, bit by bit, a feast that would have fed an eighteenth-century Bermudian sea-captain and his crew for a week, it seemed. Bread, cheese and cold meat, seafood, three kinds of salad, and two cocktail sauces. Lemon wedges, vinaigrette dressing, napkins, plates, cutlery, glasses, fruit punch. . . They didn't even discover the hors d'oeuvres until it was far too late. The glazed fruit tart dessert won over crab and mushroom canapés hands down.

Randall shrugged. 'I'll eat the canapés tomorrow for breakfast.'

'Breakfast?'

'Well. . .perhaps lunch.'

And there was champagne. He saved it until after the

mouth-watering dessert and then splashed it into the glasses until they were brimming and golden.

'This is so nice, Randall,' Summer told him. 'We ought to have a proper toast.'

'I was thinking the same,' he answered with a lazy grin.

They held their glasses up expectantly, and the liquid caught the light from the boat's cabin and sparkled against the dark backdrop of the velvety night. The perfect moment for a toast. Summer racked her brains, Randall frowned. . .and nothing came.

'Um. . . To. . . To. . .'

'To the—'

It was no good. Inspiration had flown, and after another ridiculous minute of stuttering and silence they both dissolved into laughter and agreed with no words at all just to clink their glasses together—the sound was as pure and sweet as a note of music—and drink. The champagne was light and dry, and the bubbles tickled Summer's nose and made her laugh again, and in no time both glasses were empty.

'I'm not all that fond of champagne,' Randall said, 'but tonight I could drink the whole bottle.'

'Same here. It must be a very good label.'

'Chateau Roignaix,' he shrugged, reading the Gothic print. 'I haven't heard of it, but, then. . .'

'No. The only one I can ever remember is Veuve Clicquot—'

'And I'm sure I only know *that* from James Bond films!'

'You're right!'

'Would you like some more?'

'No, I won't,' she answered him, suddenly serious, then she hesitated as she tried to explain, and the ropes clinked against the mast in the short silence. 'One glass was wonderful. It's silly, but I'm afraid that the second couldn't possibly be as good.'

'Hmm. . .' Suddenly he was standing very close to her and pulling her to her feet as he coaxed the glass out of her hand. 'And is that. . .how you feel. . .about kisses too? That the second couldn't possibly be as good? I hope not, and I hope it's not still too soon, Summer. . .'

She didn't have time to reply before his lips came to meet hers, parted with trembling expectancy although just a moment ago they had been closed. His mouth tasted of champagne, yet surely that tingling sensation couldn't still be its effervescence? His fingers cupped her face then stroked down her jaw to her neck, where they lifted the silky feathers of her dark hair so that the cool sea breeze caressed her nape.

Next he found her shoulders and slid the cream jacket down so that he could massage the bare rounded shapes, before wrapping his arms around her back and pulling her against him. Summer's own hands had taken on a life of their own as she explored the strength of his chest, waist, hips, thighs. . .

When fluting fingers reached higher again to brush beneath her breasts Summer shuddered and knew that he had felt the responsive movement. His grip tightened, his mouth parted further so that they could taste the full sweetness of each other and then they were pressed together, length to length, making her fully aware of his maleness and strength. Hungrily she pushed at his T-shirt and it came up from the waistband of his shorts so that she could feel the hot brown skin of his lower back.

His hands were still nudging at her breasts, making the sensitive tips harden and strain outwards. She sighed and took in a ragged breath that was stifled by his kiss so that she had to stretch her neck and gasp. He used the moment to paint a trail of fire the length of her throat, then he returned to her mouth once again to taste her even more deeply.

Far too soon it was over. He pulled gently away, just a little, and even that movement was sensual as the new coolness of the air heightened her tingling awareness of every nerve ending.

'Now,' he said, his lips brushing her hair then nuzzling and nibbling at her mouth again. He smiled. 'Is the second time really not as good as the first?'

'No, it's much better,' she admitted huskily, still too helplessly in the thrall of his kiss to be anything less than honest.

'And I think we'd both find that the third would be better still.'

'Mmm. . .'

'But, Summer?'

'Yes?'

He cocked his head to one side. 'Let's save the third, shall we?'

'Save it?'

'For. . . Let's just say, next time.'

'I'm disappointed.'

'You had a rough day today. John's in hospital. . .'

'John is—'

'John is a man you were engaged to just over a month ago.'

'I know. . .'

'That's not long, and I refuse to let you whisk me off to bed on our first date.' He sounded utterly convincing. 'I won't just be used for my body, OK, Summer?'

'*Randall*?'

Oh, I know what you women are like!'

'And I know what *you're* like! Completely ridiculous!'

'Just doing my best to entertain.'

'Seriously, though. . .'

'Oh, if we must. Seriously?'

'Thanks.'

'For—?'

'Being such an idiot. Making me laugh. It really helps.'

'All part of the service, ma'am.' His forefinger touched her lips. 'Now, no more.' The finger slid away, down her neat chin to her throat, and even that was a caress. 'It's getting late. Let's get you back to the marina and off home.'

'Just me?'

'I'm going to spend the night on the boat.' He had turned away from her now and was already starting to tidy away the picnic things so that the deck became again a purely functional place.

'Oh. . .'

'I'm feeling a bit restless.' He frowned.

She could see the thwarted desire tightening his limbs and stomach, and realised just how much he wanted, physically, to have her stay here with him.

She wanted it too—to sink against him once more and feel the way he supported her lighter weight with his strong frame. She wanted to tell him that it wasn't *really* their first date, that there was no need to go slowly, and that if he wanted her to stay here on the boat with him and spend the night then she would.

'I've. . .never slept on a boat,' she told him softly, giving in to the shared need that sizzled between them, 'and I promise I'll still respect you in the morning. . .'

He laughed. 'No-o, Summer. Hell, that wasn't very convincing, was it? Let me try again. *No*, Summer!'

He began to clamber around the boat, his agile feet big and brown in their old shoes and his frown heavy now as he hauled on the sheets and swung the boom across. She felt *Aquamarine* move beneath her, keeling a little as the sail filled with the cool wind and they gathered speed.

'Boom's coming round,' he warned her casually.

'Yes, OK, I see it,' she answered, ducking her head—loving his expertise.

He came briefly within reach and she laid a hand on his hard brown forearm.

'Thanks, Randall, for taking me home,' she said. 'Because, you know, I really don't want to go. That makes no sense at all, does it?'

'Yes, it does,' he answered patiently. 'So far, I have to tell you, you *always* make sense to me, Summer Westholm! It's beginning to be quite a problem.'

CHAPTER SIX

'THERE'S something very nice about taking things slowly,' Randall said as he nosed *Aquamarine* in amongst the group of tiny islands clustered in the middle of Bermuda's Great Sound.

'You mean the boat, of course,' Summer answered, watching his practised hand on the rudder, his grip relaxed yet strong.

'I mean the boat, of course,' he agreed.

But they both knew that he didn't mean the boat at all.

It was five weeks since he had first taken her sailing, and this was one of nearly a dozen excursions they had made together. A wonderful way to get to know someone, Summer considered. She was discovering in Randall Macleay the capacity to be lazy as well as vigorous, mechanical as well as medical, and meticulously tidy as well as endearingly vague. For a man who could never find his coffee-mug in a fairly small kitchen, it seemed funny that he knew exactly where each thing belonged on *Aquamarine* and each thing was always exactly in that place.

'Which beach shall we pick for breakfast?' he asked, interrupting her thoughts.

'Whichever...' They were all perfect, and it was a perfect morning.

'Well, the wind's coming straight across the water so let's not try Frog Island. We'll take a look at Pebble.'

'Fine.'

'OK, we'll need to tack.'

And she knew how to do it now. Although he hadn't

said so in so many words, he was quite definitely teaching her to sail. Not in any structured way, just in the form of an apparently offhand piece of information here and there or some easy instructions as he got her to help with something. 'This is a cleat. . . This is a winch. . . Rigging is like the workings of a bird's wing, and the sail is its feathers. . . Look, see what a bad shape I've got there? Luffing like crazy. We should be going about. Ready? Watch the boom!'

She wondered what would have happened if she hadn't enjoyed it and had resisted his, say, thrusting of a jib sheet into her hand at regular intervals, for the sake of lolling on the deck and working on her tan. Well, she didn't wonder very much. . . He wouldn't have asked her again. This was definitely a test of sorts but since she had the clear impression that she was passing it with flying colours how could she mind?

And she loved sailing, which she must have made obvious in indirect ways as he'd never actually asked her. As for the part about taking things slowly, sailing tended to keep people too busy to permit much of the elements in a relationship that were traditionally thought of as romantic.

Instead of endearments there were arcane commands like, 'Hard a'lee!' and, instead of gazing into his blue eyes, she spent far more time gazing ahead at the dark jade waters of the Great Sound, trying to remember what he had said about red and green buoys.

It was so *right* of him to handle it this way, though, that she felt herself falling for him far more deeply, entwining herself to him far more closely than she might have done if they'd taken the opposite route and spent all of their time in bed. As yet, they hadn't done *that* at all, and in her black moments, starting to feel ready for it, she did wonder, Maybe he's not serious. Maybe he's just looking for crew, or trying to make me feel at home in Bermuda.

There were certain antidotes to this negative way of thinking, however—his kisses, for example, which generally came just at the right moment. Like now. . .

He had used the speed left in the boat to ease as close to the tiny pale pink scallop of beach as possible, and then dropped a lightweight anchor and let out enough rope to make the pull on it as close to horizontal as he could.

'. . .which means we'll be swimming to breakfast.'

'A new experience for me,' she answered gravely.

'Thought it might be. So far you've shown an admirable enthusiasm for them. Hope this isn't a stretch. . .'

'When it must be nearly eighty degrees already, and I've had my swimming costume on under my shorts all morning? Definitely not!'

Which was when he kissed her, taking her by surprise just as she reached to cross her arms and lift her T-shirt over her head so that his hands slid all the way up her bare arms and then trapped them against her body. 'Mmm, yes, you're very warm,' he said, then grazed her mouth. 'Even your lips. . .'

'They must be dry from the salt and the wind.'

'Not at all.'

Neither were his. A little salty, yes, but deliciously so, and the taste and the surrounding flavour of the sea reminded her that she was hungry. Well. . .not all that hungry. As his kiss deepened she forgot about that sensation again and concentrated on this one. Hands threading into the satiny feathers of her hair, hips bumping gently against her and the hard, shallow curves of his thighs locking with her own softer flesh.

Finally, though, 'We've only got two hours before we'll have to weigh anchor or lose the tide,' he said.

'Oh, only that?' she answered wistfully, although most people might have have considered that quite a reasonable amount of time in which to eat breakfast.

'At this spot, Summer,' he came in quickly. 'As far as I'm concerned, we've got the whole day to go other places.'

Or even the night? It was there in the air between them and in the sudden hungry urgency of his mouth on hers, but neither of them put the awareness into words.

'How are we going to get our breakfast to shore?' she asked as he released her at last.

'I'll float it on a life-raft. It's specially packed in a vessel that will minimise the possibility of salt-water contamination.'

Since he had insisted on providing the meal himself, she hadn't seen it yet and laughed when he produced the red plastic bucket.

'You've got to admit, it's leakproof,' he pointed out indignantly.

'Unless it capsizes.'

'I haven't capsized a vessel in years!'

He didn't this time, either, and they were soon both ashore on the small, uninhabited beach, with towels spread to sit on.

Here, in the sheltered waters of the Sound, the waves were merely a rhythmic little frill of lace, frothing against the sand, and he'd gauged the wind correctly so that the beach he had chosen was sheltered from the breeze.

Summer got out her sunblock cream. She had done her face and hands and legs before they set out from the marina, but now her shoulders and neck and upper back were bare as well. Pooling the white cream into her hand and spreading it across her skin, she saw that Randall was watching, his smile lazily sensual, and her breath caught in her throat for a moment.

He wasn't offering to do this for her, but he might as well have done. His eyes were like fingers, caressing her as they took in every inch of her skin, and if he wasn't sending her telepathic messages about how his hands would feel on her then it must be an exceptionally creative element in her own imagination that was producing these vivid images.

He was *still* watching her. Capping the cream again, she raised her eyebrows and he said very soberly, 'I'm glad to see you're aware of the dangers of skin cancer, that's all. I'm just ogling my approval.'

'Is that what it is? You're not going to see me sporting a tan, though.'

'I love your creamy skin.'

'You wouldn't prefer me golden brown?'

'All shiny and tough like leather, you mean? We do get some serious tanners here still, all nicely marinated in their cocoa butter. They make me think of advertisements for rotisserie chicken.'

'Ugh!'

'Yes, it's enough to put you off for life, isn't it?'

'Off tanning?'

'Off chicken.'

'Is that what we're having?'

'Nothing so elaborate, I'm afraid.'

But the simplicity of slippery tropical fruit, rolls, butter, jam and cheese, with coffee as well, felt just right out here in the open as the sun dried their swimsuits and heated their skin.

Summer felt so lazy after their brisk sail that she didn't try to talk, just ate and watched the water. . .and Randall. Then she caught him watching her again, but this time there was something serious in his face, and after a minute she realised that he was working up to something.

She cocked her head questioningly to one side, frowned at him and then smiled enquiringly. 'Randall?'

'Just wondering. . . Did you know John came to see me last week?'

'He did?' It wasn't what she had expected at all and, as always, she felt a little awkward about discussing her former fiancé. He had had several days in hospital after his dramatic descent into ketoacidosis five weeks ago and she had been twice more to see him, each time hoping vainly that there would be some sign of Alex. As far as she'd been able to tell, there was nothing, not even a card, and she wondered, Is it just because John wouldn't have her told? Or is he right? She just couldn't handle his disease. I'm *sure* he still cares for her!

After his release from hospital he had had several appointments with Steve at the centre, but had said nothing to Summer about how he was coping and had not turned up at any classes or support group sessions, although she knew that Steve had suggested both. And now, for some reason, he had been to see Randall.

'You were up at the hospital, I think,' Randall was saying. 'I didn't know if he would have told you himself.'

'He didn't, no. I—haven't seen him, except when he's been in to see Steve, and even then. . . Well, you know there's not much time to talk when we have a full appointment schedule.'

'He's asked to switch from Steve to me.'

'Oh. Was—was Steve upset?' She didn't know quite what to say.

Randall shrugged. 'It happens. It's best if someone can be seen by the doctor they feel most comfortable with. In this case. . .' He sighed. 'John's still casting about for easy answers. Steve didn't have any. Now he hopes that I will.'

'And do you?'

'Of course not! I may suggest that he tries a jet injector, since the injections themselves seem to bother him a lot.'

'Yes, they have done from the beginning.' Summer nodded, remembering the long sessions of practice John had gone through in hospital in London months ago—

injecting an orange until it was perforated with holes, then the agonising ten minutes or more that he took to work himself up to giving the shot into his own flesh, tensing his muscles so that, in the end, the pain was worse.

'But I do feel awkward, Summer.'

'Because I was engaged to him. . .?'

He nodded, and there was an uncomfortable little silence. Hating it, she tried to break it with humour and teased, 'What, you're jealous?'

'Actually, yes.'

The response startled her into laughter, then she saw that he was serious and exclaimed, 'Randall, that's absurd!'

'Isn't it, though? What on earth would I have to be jealous of?' he mocked. 'Me, a humble doctor, who'd probably be happier living in a boat instead of a house, jealous of someone who's wealthy, involved in a glamorous profession and a good ten years younger than I am.'

'Now, *are* you serious? I don't believe it!'

'No. . . Yes! Not really. Just. . .curious, perhaps, about what went wrong between the two of you. And a little afraid that you and I have met at the wrong time.'

'Because I'm not over John?'

'Perhaps. It can be more complicated than that.'

'True, I suppose. As to what went wrong, it was more a case of not ever being *right*.'

'Really?'

'I. . .wouldn't have made a good wife to him, Randall, despite the obvious advantages of it.'

Staring down at her nails and badly wanting to chew at one of them—perhaps that well-shaped, appetising-looking crescent jutting just over the edge of her left thumb—she thought of the luxurious Giangrande residence in Bermuda, Olivewood House, that John had shown her pictures of, although she hadn't actually seen it.

Attending parties, wearing designer clothes, hosting celebrity visitors, always being on show. . .

'It's the kind of thing people assume they could handle,' she told Randall, still not looking at him. 'We all tell ourselves, ''Of course I would!'' but how many of us could, really?' She was thinking aloud, not explaining herself very clearly, and realised it after a moment and looked up at last to apologise. 'Sorry, that didn't make any sense, did it?' Her thumb-nail, miraculously, was still intact.

'I'm not sure if it did or not,' he answered slowly, and there was an odd look on his face, as if—unpleasant image, but it fitted—he'd just taken a large gulp of his coffee to find that the milk had turned but he was too well mannered to spit it out.

They lay there for a few minutes more. The conversation seemed to have limped to a halt, snagged raggedly on the subject of John. Summer told herself that of course it couldn't be tension-free, having a nice chat with one's soon-to-be-lover about one's erstwhile fiancé when the former was the latter's doctor.

I won't keep on about it, she thought. Enough's been said. It'll take time, and even then perhaps it's just not meant to be.

But that was a sensible conclusion which left her feeling very deflated and unhappy as he began to pack the remains of their meal back into the red bucket, while muttering darkly about the tide.

They had a swim, and that seemed to help. The water was so perfect! Cool enough to be refreshing and warm enough to keep them there for half an hour—swimming or floating lazily, splashing each other, diving for shells.

'You said you weren't wealthy, Randall, but you are, as far as I'm concerned,' she told him. 'Rich in the things that matter—like a career you love, a family home, beauty all around you.'

'Well, yes, that's how I usually think of it. I'm glad you said that, Summer.'

Then the tide really was threatening to desert them so they weighed anchor and set their sails again.

'I was thinking you'd like to see the spinnaker in action today,' he said when they were clear of the islands.

'Yes, please.'

So they did that for two hours, had a bit more to eat—salads, this time, and juice—and then started back to the marina, and if Summer had been right earlier about the tension in the air it was definitely gone now.

'You did a good job, packing that genoa sail away,' Randall told her when *Aquamarine* was securely moored again and most of the gear was shipshape and stored away.

'I like acquiring new skills,' she answered lightly. 'You never know when they might come in handy. Like riding a bicycle or playing bridge or, um. . .'

'Changing a nappy?'

'Exactly. You never know when it might suddenly be extremely convenient to be able to say, "Oh, you're stowing a genoa? Here, let me!"'

He laughed, and then frowned up at the older man who had suddenly appeared above them on the jetty. 'Hi, Tom.'

'Thought it was you, Dr Macleay.' He was breathless. 'We've got a problem. Can you come?'

'Sure. Medical, you mean?'

'Yes. Fellow in the group that's hired our big motor cruiser for the afternoon. He's collapsed and he doesn't seem to be breathing, they say. I've called the ambulance, but—'

Randall lunged up onto the dock above his mooring. With the tide at low ebb now, it should have been an awkward movement but somehow it wasn't. Summer was just wondering how she would cover the same distance when he turned to reach down and haul her up. 'We'll need you too.'

Tom was leading the way, lumbering along at a rapid clip. 'Hell, I hope it's not serious! They'd only just gone out. Six of them. All older men, wanting some fishing. When they turned around I thought there must be a problem with the boat. Ed Tucker's a good skipper. . .'

'Was he eating?' Randall demanded.

'Ed?'

'The ill man.'

'Choking, you think? God, I've got no details. I was out on the dock. Ed didn't try to radio in, just came straight around. They were all yelling at me before they even moored. Here—'

The big white cruiser was moored now and a group of five men, all in their late sixties or possibly older, was gathered around the uniformed skipper, who was bent over the lumpy figure on the deck and tentatively performing CPR.

'Here's Doc Macleay, Ed,' Tom called.

'Thank God! Doc, I think it's too late. . .I did the course in CPR, but when it's the real thing. . .'

'You did what you could,' Randall said, then wasted no more time in talk.

He checked the motionless man's airway first and found it clear then immediately went on with the cardiopulmonary resuscitation that Ed Tucker had tried, but with none of the skipper's gentleness. His thumps on the man's chest were brutal in their force and relentless in their rhythm, and there were gasps and hisses from the other men.

'Steady on, you'll break his ribs.'

'Yes, and save his life, I hope,' was all Randall spared the time to say. 'Someone get my medical kit from the boat. Tom?'

'Stowed in the galley?'

'Yes, under the starboard seat.'

'Right.'

Randall's shoulders rippled, and his eyes never left the man's form. Summer knew what she had to do as well. She positioned herself at his head and began mouth-to-mouth resuscitation, while feeling for the carotid artery along his neck to check for any sign of a pulse.

'Got it?' Randall asked.

'Yes, but—' The doctor's thumping stopped for a moment and Summer felt again. 'Nothing now,' she told him. 'Keep going.'

Again, those violent pumpings. She heard the crack of a rib, and another. The man was elderly, probably in his late sixties, and his bones had acquired the typical brittleness of age. 'What's his history—does anyone know?' Randall barked.

Three voices began at once, volunteering a cacophony of detail that was incomprehensible. 'One at a time,' Randall decreed. 'You!' He pointed to a man whose features were twisted with concern.

'I've known Dick for years. He's never mentioned heart trouble, though he did have high blood pressure for a while when he was smoking. I— Damn, I should be able to tell you more!'

'Don't worry. We're working in the dark, then. OK, try that pulse again, Summer.' He sat back, breathless now from the intense labour, and she held her breath as her fingertips quested for a continuation of the vital rhythm which would show that the heart was pumping on its own.

'Yes. . .' she said after a few seconds. 'Thready, though. Very weak.'

'OK, more, then.' He went back to work for long seconds more, and Summer could see that he was tiring. Sweat had broken out on his forehead, his neck glistened with it and his T-shirt was starting to cling and darken. The rhythm and pressure weren't quite so dramatic and violent now.

'Take a break, Randall,' she urged him quietly. 'Let Ed Tucker have another try. You're starting to ease up too much.'

'Am I? Hell!' He ignored her suggestion and renewed his efforts, his face twisted now and cords standing out on his neck, then sat back again at last. 'How's that pulse?' They could all hear how breathless he was.

'Doc, let me have another—' Ed Tucker began.

'Hang on, it's steady,' Summer said urgently. 'Yes, still steady. Randall, I think you've done it.'

Tom had arrived with the medical kit from *Aquamarine* and Randall pulled out his stethoscope and listened to the man's chest. 'Yes! Thank God, that rhythm is holding now, and his breathing is. . .shallow. Still very weak. Summer, let me take over there.'

Seeing how breathless he was, she wanted to protest, but saw the total determination and involvement in his face so moved quickly aside and he gave mouth-to-mouth now, holding his own ragged breathing steady by sheer force of will. She saw the sweat-dampened strands of hair that curled on his neck, ached to touch him there and realised, I love him. How can that be? It's true, though. I love him.

She was so consumed with the realisation that she almost didn't register the keening of the ambulance's siren, until the vehicle nosed slowly down the boat ramp and onto the dock, able to come almost alongside the big white cruiser.

'Take over again, Summer,' Randall said. 'I'm going to put up a drip right now.'

The ambulance officers responded quickly to his tersely worded orders, and he had soon inserted a line through which to infuse normal saline as well as drugs to stimulate the heart and control the pain which Dick Acton would feel as soon as he came to consciousness. Summer helped to fit an oxygen mask, and then the ambulance officers slid him onto a stretcher and into the gaping rear of the vehicle, while Randall filled them in on as much detail as he could.

A few moments later the ambulance was on its way.

The remaining five men were subdued, as were Ed and Tom. 'Hell, Dr Macleay,' the latter muttered. 'The sound of those ribs. . .'

'Only two, I think,' Randall answered. 'It can't be helped. You saw, didn't you, that I couldn't have used less force? He's alive now and, from what I can work out of the timing, he was out for less than the critical four minutes. A narrow shave, though.'

'Thank God you were here!'

There was a silence now after the drama. People didn't seem quite sure what to do. Summer saw Ed cast Tom a questioning look, and Tom answered with a shrug. Was the fishing trip off now? Summer assumed that it would be, and was too full of her new knowledge about the depth of her feeling for Randall to do more than stand there—drained by her part in saving Dick Acton's life, exultant about what she felt, fearful of its power and awed by the miracle of a life saved.

Then the silence was broken. 'Er. . . As long as you're here, Doc,' began a bluff, over-tanned man in Bermuda shorts so loud that they were positively operatic.

'Yes?' Randall turned to him politely.

'Would you have a look at this spot on my skin for me? It's not a mello-nomia, is it?'

'A *what*?'

'You know, the skin cancer. Mello-nomia. Here, look, this mole here.'

'I'm not a skin specialist, Mr. . .'

'Tony. Tony Gilroy.'

'. . .Mr Gilroy, nor an oncologist.'

'Eh?'

'A cancer doctor.'

'Oh, I'm not asking for free treatment, if that's what you're worried about. Just have a look and, tell you what, I'll buy you a beer. *Two* beers if you tell me there's something wrong with it.' He chuckled. 'Can't say fairer than that!'

The accent was broad yet indeterminate. Summer suspected that Australians, New Zealanders and South Africans would all be equally afraid that he was a compatriot and equally eager to disown him.

Randall was maintaining a stoical politeness as Tony Gilroy turned, raised a lemon-yellow knit shirt and started scrabbling at the middle of his back with awkwardly placed fingers. 'Now, where is the damn thing?'

Randall stepped forward and touched a loose, harmless-looking pinkish-brown area just next to the spine. 'If you mean this. . .'

'Hang on, put my finger on it. *Without* breaking my arm, if you can!' Randall obeyed, a little grim-faced now. 'Yeah, that's it. It feels a bit funny, see.'

'It looks fine to me, Mr Gilroy.'

'Are you sure?'

'Quite sure. It's what's called a skin tag, technically not a mole at all, and it doesn't appear to be irritated or inflamed.'

'No, well. . .I might get it looked at properly when I get home. As you say, you're not a skin specialist or an anchiologist. I'll be at the Harbour Links Hotel tonight, so come by for that beer.'

'Thanks for the invitation,' Randall drawled, but any sarcasm was lost on Tony Gilroy.

He was chuckling at his companions. 'Easy way to earn a drink, I'd say! Now, where's our skipper? We should head out again if we're to have a chance at those marlin.'

'I won't, if you don't mind, Tony,' said a white-haired but very fit-looking American, the man who had been so upset at not knowing more of his friend's medical history. 'I want to get to the hospital as soon as possible to find out how Dick's doing.'

'Me too,' said another member of the party.

'I'd still be up for it,' said someone else. 'I mean, I doubt they'll let us in to see Dick yet, and he and I are just acquaintances, after all. He wouldn't expect me to give up this day on his account.'

'No, I agree with Andy,' said the last man.

'Well, that's amicably settled, then,' drawled the white-haired American.

But Tony Gilroy wasn't satisfied yet. 'Hang on, though, Paul, that means the rest of us'll be up for. . .what, an extra hundred and fifty bucks apiece for the boat rental.'

'Tony, I really don't think, under the circumstances, that we'll mind chipping in our share. In fact, I'll pay for the whole thing, if you like,' Paul offered patiently, clearly having his tolerance stretched very thin.

'Well, that's very generous of you, Paul!'

The group split up, and Randall and Summer took advantage of the momentary confusion to slip away back to *Aquamarine* to finish stowing the gear and retrieve wet towels and picnic remnants.

'You must have been tempted to tell him it *was* a melanoma,' Summer said once they were out of earshot of the group.

'Oh, no, my friend! I was going to invent a much longer and more terrifying word than that,' he answered.

Then they realised that the white-haired American, Paul,

had caught up behind them and must have overheard.

'Look, we didn't thank you properly in all the drama,' he said.

'Not to worry,' was Randall's answer. 'He's alive. That'll do for thanks. And he may not thank me for those cracked ribs and all the bruises!'

'No, but seriously.' He produced a cheque-book. 'You must have a fee. . .'

'For restarting stuck hearts?'

'This is awkward. . . Tony Gilroy was crass just then and, believe me, I'm trying not to be the same, but I know how it is. I'm a stockbroker by trade, and the way I get buttonholed and pressured for free market advice at parties sometimes. . . You saved my friend's life just now—'

'Didn't take long,' Randall pointed out cheerfully.

'All right. I won't press the point. But thank you again.' He wrung Randall's hand with sincere warmth. 'And here's my card.' He took a white rectangle out of his wallet. 'If you're ever in New York, please call. And I mean that!'

'Just do one thing for me,' Randall said.

'Yes, of course. What is it?'

'Stick by your friend. He's in for a long haul.'

'You don't have to tell me! My father went through it twenty years ago.'

They talked for a few minutes more then Paul Bailey left them again, his bearing very upright and capable as he walked back along the dock.

Summer said when he had gone, 'People are funny, aren't they?'

'You mean it takes all sorts? Even sorts like Tony Gilroy?'

'Yes.'

'But wouldn't it be boring if everyone was as impeccably brought up and beautifully behaved as me?'

'Oh, Randall, you really are—'

'Awful,' he calmly agreed.

They were trembling on the brink of a consummation. They both felt it that night, although the new knowledge of the depth of what she felt was something that vibrated inside Summer, unspoken. After leaving *Aquamarine* secure at her moorings with all gear stowed, they drifted back to Randall's place with no particular plan—just some freshly bought fish and the tacit knowledge that they wanted to be together.

Summer showered off the salt water and put on the fresh linen shorts and matching blouse she'd packed in her beach-bag that morning, then went out into the garden to find that he had seasoned the fish and wrapped in it foil, as well as starting the barbecue coals.

'What else is there to bring out?' she asked.

He made a face. 'That's it, I'm afraid. Bread and butter and lemon, and I've rustled up half an avocado each to go with it. No salad, no dessert. Not exactly a gourmet feast.'

'But the fish is fresh and the wine is cold and the evening is gorgeous,' she answered.

'Thanks for your tact!'

'I mean it, Randall. Where's the sense in shutting yourself away in some stuffy restaurant, eating a heavy meal with too many courses, when there's this?' She waved her hand at the view of the Great Sound and its frame of blooming hibiscus in pink, red, white and yellow.

'You don't like restaurants?'

She shrugged apologetically. 'Not really. They make things so elaborate and sometimes you have to sit there for hours. Usually I've got other things to do!' And I'd rather be alone, just with you, although I'm not brave enough to say that yet.

He laughed. 'Then the fact that, of the numerous meals

we've had together now, none have been at a restaurant of any description. . .'

'Hasn't bothered me at all,' she finished for him. There was a silence, in which their eyes met and held, and she was aware of every inch of her skin under his caressing scrutiny.

The fish in its foil packet was on the grill now, and Randall sprawled lazily on the grass. He had set out a wrought-iron garden chair for her but she felt stiff and awkward, sitting in it alone, and got up restlessly to go and pick some of the oleander blossom that grew against the old water-tank.

'Careful,' he told her. 'The sap is extremely poisonous.'

'Is it? Such a lovely thing? It's everywhere, too.' She drew back, and did not touch the pink-blooming shrub after all.

Instead, she wandered to the brazier, and caught the sizzle of the fish and the savoury aroma that was seeping out of the shiny foil. Then, somehow, she was lying on the grass as well, close enough to touch Randall through she did not dare.

But he made it easy for her, rolling lazily so that his hand. . .just his hand. . .could reach her hair. Her fingers tangled the soft dark strands and he murmured something that she didn't quite hear, but to prompt him to repeat it. . .? No. Her voice just wouldn't work. Her senses, all of them, were far too distracted by the simple yet utterly sensual play of his fingers.

Now he had found the tender skin behind her ears and her nape, where her hair was even finer. She closed her eyes, quite hypnotised, until she heard his low plea, 'Aren't you going to come any closer, Summer?'

'Randall. . .' She was stretched beside him, without knowing how she had got there, and then he was kissing her hungrily.

His mouth was hot and hard, demanding a response as strong as his own—and it was incredibly easy to give it. Half his weight was on her now. The pressure was heavy and confining and yet it was meltingly sweet and welcome too.

Her lips had parted, and she found that he tasted of the fresh wine that she herself had sipped. Letting her eyes drift shut, she felt his fingers rake once more through her hair then he rolled again so that she was on top of him, still a prisoner of his sensuous hands as they moved to trace again and again the shallow S-shaped curve that ran from her spine to her thighs. She opened her eyes a little, needing to see him, and through the screen of her lashes those rare grey threads in his dark hair were like silver in the late rays of the sun.

Their kiss seemed to last for hours until, finally, she said breathlessly through swollen lips, 'Randall, I must be crushing you.'

'Crushing me? You're a feather. Come, stay. . .stay!'

Her resistance was only a token and she sank her head onto the hard plateau of his chest, as if sinking into the most comfortable bed in the world. There! She could hear his heartbeat, quickened by his arousal. The primal rhythm was strong and regular beneath the angular shape of is pectoral muscle. She moved her head slightly so that it was pillowed on his shoulder, and now she could trace the tanned column of his throat with her fingers and marvel at the silkiness of the hair that patterned his chest above the open-necked blue shirt.

The sun had gone now and it was evening. With a delicious sense that time didn't matter in the slightest, she asked lazily, 'Would the fish be done, do you think?'

'Hungry?'

'Getting that way. Wouldn't want it to spoil. Really fresh fish is such a treat.'

The fish *was* done, lopsidedly so since it hadn't been turned on its grill. The bottom was quite crisp and golden and almost about to burn, while the top was so moist and tender and fresh that it was almost sweet. With the other simple ingredients it was a perfect and satisfying meal, and by the end of it darkness had fallen.

'Want to go in?' he asked.

'Not particularly,' she answered.

'No. . . It's nice out, isn't it?'

'Nice? It's heaven! You Bermudians do take your weather for granted!' She licked the last of the tangy mixture of salt, butter and lemon from her fingers as she spoke.

'Stop that!' he growled suddenly.

'What?'

'Licking your fingers.'

'Why? I haven't been touching the oleander.' She was almost alarmed at his threatening tone, and wiped her hands quickly on a paper napkin.

'No, but something much more dangerous is happening.'

'Good heavens, I—'

'I can't stand to have your fingers on the receiving end of it, Summer,' he groaned, and before she realised what he was doing he had scooped her from the grass into his arms and made masterfully sure that it was his own mouth that took the benediction of her lips and tongue.

Dangerous. . . He had already used the word. The night had enclosed them now, the darkness like a cocoon around them and the balmy air a caress—too mild even for dew. Like some tropical passion-flower that blossomed after the sun had set, she felt herself opening to him, her mouth almost bruised—but deliciously so—from his kiss, and the most sensuous core of her body throbbing at every touch of skin to skin.

When he pulled her down to the silky grass again she knew what he wanted. How could she not have known? Every inch of her wanted it too, and both of them were saying so with each touch of lips or fingers, and each pressure of thigh to thigh and tingling breasts to rapidly rising and falling chest. He pulled the peacock-blue shirt over his head with one supple, rippling movement and her fingers splayed to press against his chest then slide to his back, glorying in the contours of hard muscle and soft skin, cool hair and warm flesh.

For many more minutes their bodies moved feverishly together, then suddenly the urgency departed and there was a lull, a slow, sensous few moments in which he lay beside her, his firm mouth very serious as his fingers drifted to the small buttons on her blouse and carefully unfastened them, the back of his hand brushing with deliberate, feather-light strokes against the swell of her breasts bared to the evening air above the lacy cups of her cream satin bra.

He unfastened that, too, with enough clumsiness—and a muttered curse—to tell her that this *wasn't* something he did every day with a passing parade of women. A moment later she was bared to him and she felt the delicious tightening of her skin at the anticipation of his touch. First he kissed her, then reached to trace the two curves of tender flesh that fell like taut pillows towards the grass as she lay on her side. She strained against him and wound her arms around his back, burying her face in his neck so that her moan of pleasure was stifled by his warm, muscled flesh.

They stayed like that until she was aching, and so dizzy with the awareness of his touch that she almost didn't understand when he whispered, 'Are you. . .taking some kind of precautions?'

'Hmm?' She lay still as his fingers plaited their magic

on her breasts, shoulders, neck. It was hard to really listen to what he was saying.

'You know what I mean.'

'Oh. . . Um. . .'

'Babies, Summer. This is how they happen, you know. . .'

'Yes, I'm sorry, Randall, I wasn't thinking. . .' She moved away, chilled at her own irresponsibility, and wrapped her arms around her own naked torso instead of his.

'I know,' he said gently, 'but there's no need to stiffen like that.' He coaxed her back to him. 'I was just asking.'

'But I'm *not*—taking precautions, I mean. I just hadn't thought that far ahead.'

'I see.' Now he was the one who had tensed, and his withdrawal was complete. He sat up, hugging his knees and with the wide expanse of his back shielding his expression from her.

'Randall?' She touched him on the shoulder and he flinched.

She drew her hand back with a gasp and he said quickly, 'Sorry. I'm not angry. We'll have to stop, that's all. I'm not the kind of man that could forge ahead regardless, as you should know by now.'

'Yes, I do know it, Randall. It's just I'm not experienced enough to have premeditated this.' She tried to make light of it, but didn't fully succeed. 'I never went along with the notion of free love that people like my parents are supposed to have gone for—although, in fact, they didn't! And it didn't occur to me to. . .um. . .pop something in my purse when I left home this morning for a sailing breakfast.'

'Of course it didn't,' he growled. 'Me neither, although I wish pretty desperately that it had!' He turned to her again and added quickly, through clenched teeth,

'Summer, can you put your clothes back on, please?'

'Oh. . .' She blushed as she followed his hungry gaze to the pale, shadowy shapes of her breasts above the linen shorts. Their dusky pink peaks tautened once again as she was all too aware of what he wanted to do.

A few moments later they were both fully clothed again, having dressed in an awkward silence. Now she stood, uncertain of what he wanted from her.

'I should go,' she said tentatively, her heart in her throat. He didn't seem angry, but he had retreated somehow. 'It's late.'

'It isn't. . . Don't go,' he growled. '*Please* don't! Come inside and have coffee. Hell, I don't want you to feel that you're not wanted now!'

'*Am* I wanted, then?' Scarcely aware of the movement, she came towards him—needing to touch him, needing to hear something of her own newly realised feelings put into his words. But he backed away from the uncertain reach of her hand.

'Careful, Summer. Damn it! Don't expect miracles from me. I may be responsible but I am a man, and this garden is too damned perfect a setting tonight. And that couch inside is pretty comfortable, too. So perhaps you're right. Let's not make this a challenge we can't win. I'd better drop you home.'

'Mmm,' she nodded, already gathering her bag.

She saw that he was piling the scraps from their meal into the cold, torn piece of foil that had held the fish.

He dropped her at her flat in Paget half an hour later, after a kiss which neither of them had dared to prolong for more than a moment but which offered more promise than she'd known a kiss could contain.

Nothing had been said about love by either of them, she realised as she listened to the sound of his car ebbing into the night, but perhaps, as yet, it didn't need to be.

CHAPTER SEVEN

MAYA GIANGRANDE came into the diabetes care centre on Wednesday morning the following week—a week that, so far, had been full of secret, shared moments between herself and Randall although they'd both been too busy to see each other outside work. Summer hadn't seen Maya since a very brief chance encounter in Hamilton one Saturday morning well over a month ago, and as always she found her efficient, confident manner slightly abrasive.

'I should have made the time for this weeks ago,' she said to Summer. 'But you know how it is. The height of the tourist season. And, of course, Alex Page's departure from Rose Beach has left us scrambling there. We didn't realise quite how capable she was until we lost her to our Bahamas resort so I hope they appreciate her!'

'Alex Page has left?' Summer heard herself say blankly.

It wasn't remotely what they were supposed to be talking about. Maya had come in to see Dr Macleay and to have a lesson in siting her shots of the newer purified insulin she was now using so that the depressions beneath her skin, particularly on her thighs, would slowly start to fill in. With a full morning herself, and a class and a support group meeting in the afternoon and early evening, Summer didn't have the leisure for a gossip session but of course Maya was now answering her blurted question, surprised.

'You didn't *know*?'

'Not at all. . .'

'How stupid of me, then! I assumed. . . Well, I assumed that John would have told you. I actually—forgive me—

wondered if you might have had something to do with it.'

'But why would you think it was any of my concern?' Summer asked blankly, unsettled as she had been before by Maya's frankness. 'Surely you know. . . Our engagement has been broken for nearly two months.'

'Yes, but isn't that *why* it was broken?' Maya returned. 'Because of Alex? I thought you might have issued him some kind of ultimatum. . .'

'No, not at all. It was—' Summer hesitated, not wanting to open herself up any further. True, Alex Page had been a catalyst of sorts, making Summer realise that she and John didn't love each other, but this wasn't what Maya was implying now. She said firmly, 'It was something else entirely.'

Maya stared at her, her dark eyes narrowed, and Summer could see that the cogs were whirring. And since she absolutely *didn't* want to continue this conversation. . .'But you're here for professional advice, so let's not keep you for too long over this, shall we? Here's a syringe. Now, this is all you need to do. . .'

Five minutes later Maya was called in to see Randall, and that was the end of it, but Summer was left with an uneasy feeling. How many other people, in the Giangrande family and out of it, were speculating about what had happened between herself and John? And what mistaken conclusions had they reached? She had thought by this time that it was all over and done with. Why did anyone feel that they had a right to know?

She was upset that Alex had transferred to the Bahamas, too. She really loved John, I know she did, and he loved her. If he didn't at least try to rekindle their relationship then he's let diabetes shape his life in a way that didn't have to be, and yet I'm in the worst possible position to do anything about that!

Her next patient was ready, and then she was due up

at the hospital to talk to a new type two patient about oral hypoglycaemics and self-monitoring of blood glucose. She was aware now, as she took sixty-two-year-old Mrs Mathieson's observations and dealt with a potentially troublesome callus on her foot, that Randall was spending a long time with Maya today, considering it was a very routine check-up. She was collecting her things, ready to go up to the hospital, when the two of them emerged at last, and Mrs Mathieson had been waiting to see Randall for several minutes.

'He'll only be a moment more now,' she reassured the older woman, then heard Maya's confident, carrying voice.

'Again, as I say, I'm getting very worried about how down he is, and now that he's seeing you. . .'

'Thanks,' Randall answered. 'What you said. . .certainly bears a lot of thinking about.'

There was something oddly strained about his tone—an obvious reserve—and from his words and Maya's it seemed clear that they had been discussing John.

It's too close-knit! Summer thought. He shouldn't have been discussing one patient with another, even if they are close relatives and have the same disease. Is that why he looks so stiff and cold? Maya said far more than he wanted her to, and he couldn't fob her off?

She looked at him, able to see his profile as she moved to let herself out of the side door. His face was so tight!

Then the door clicked as she opened it and he turned in time to see her. But there was no private smile as he registered her presence, no acknowledgment at all of the heat that had been simmering between them, more intense than ever since the weekend—just that stiff face and blue eyes that were almost burning. She made a tiny, lurching step towards him, needing to know what the matter was, why he was so. . .upset? Angry? But before she could speak he had turned away again and was striding towards the waiting-room.

'I'll see you now, Mrs Mathieson,' he said, and Summer could only get on with her own schedule.

Penny Malley was browsing through a rack of pamphlets in the waiting-room when Summer returned from the hospital to collect her sandwich lunch. 'Can I take some of these, Summer?'

'Yes, of course, go ahead. Take whatever you want. They're for anyone who needs them.'

It was true, and yet a bit of a fob-off. She was planning to go up to the botanical gardens with her sandwich and had no desire to cut her break short. Randall was at the hospital himself at the moment, although she hadn't run into him there, and there was a nagging intuition which told her that she didn't want a snatched encounter with him today.

They'd been planning to go out together tonight after her support group meeting finished at seven, and unvoiced between them was the awareness that it would probably be the night they would make love for the first time. After their talk the other night and their shared struggle to keep some vestige of good sense against the clamourings of physical need, she had even been to see a local doctor to arrange for contraception. Let her be patient until tonight, then, so that if there was something odd going on they'd have a proper chance to talk about it and their so-important first night together would not be ruined.

So now she hesitated. If she hung back, talking to Penny, and Randall appeared again when they'd only be able to exchange the briefest of words. . .

And yet she was very curious about Penny's request. The young woman had been dealing with her diabetes for years. Surely these glossy, simply written pamphlets with titles such as 'Diabetes and You' could have little new to tell her now.

'Was there anything particular you were interested in?'

'Well, yes, this one looked good. ''What is Type One Diabetes?'' And these ones about diet and meal-planning. But I was wondering if there was anything aimed at friends and relatives of diabetics.'

'Here.' Summer came across to the rack. 'This green one, and this one here. . .' she pulled another slim folded brochure from the top of the rack '. . .give a good introduction for people who don't know much about the disease.'

She thought she knew, now, what Penny wanted the pamphlets for.

'You've told Larry, then?' she added eagerly. 'And he wants to know more about it?'

But Penny made a face. 'No, I haven't told him yet. I'm going to tonight. He's coming over to my place early, before Mum and Dad get home from work, and I'm going to cook him an extra-nice dinner to show that really I can eat almost anything I want. Then I'll give him these pamphlets because they can explain it all better than I could. Then, if he wants to, I'll show him how I prick the side of my finger to test my blood glucose—which I've got down to a fine art now—and even my evening insulin shot, if he wants to see that. What do you think? A pretty good plan, isn't it?'

Summer's heart sank at the young woman's poignant mixture of optimism and doubt. 'I don't know, Penny,' she said gently. 'I don't know him, do I? But perhaps it would be better *not* to plan it, don't you think? To wait until there's a moment that seems really right.'

'No. . .' Penny shook her head, her face suddenly tight and stubborn. 'If I think that way I might procrastinate for weeks more, and it's getting to the point where he *has* to know. We're spending such a lot of time together that

I can't go on hiding all the paraphernalia. With this new plan Dr Macleay worked out with me, I'm injecting four times a day and testing blood sugar that often too. That makes an awful lot of unexplained disappearing into the bathroom. Not to mention that if I had an insulin reaction he ought to know the signs and what to do about it in case I don't recognise it myself. . .and sometimes I don't.'

'Yes. . .' Summer murmured.

'I'm a planning sort of person, you see, and of course diabetes tends to intensify that trait. No, this is definitely the best way. . . And I think I'll take this one on diabetes and travel, too, because he was talking about a trip to New York.' She laughed and blushed prettily. 'He wasn't very specific, but it almost sounded as if he was talking about a honeymoon!'

She left the centre on light feet, with the wad of pamphlets fluttering brightly in her hand, and Summer went across for her curtailed lunch break in the botanical gardens, her mind dwelling on Penny now as well as Randall and that difficult conversation with Maya this morning about John.

I hope Penny's not setting herself up for a bad fall, Summer thought.

The fact that, underneath, she's so anxious about this, so determined to prove to him that diabetes won't matter. . . It almost sounds as if she knows he'll have problems with it. . .

And suddenly she was thinking about Alex Page again, too. Could that be why she was in the Bahamas now? Perhaps John *had* tried to rekindle his relationship with her and she hadn't, after all, been able to handle the prospect of his lifelong routine of blood-sugar control. And if John was 'down', as Maya had said to Randall, that could well be why.

This personal concern gave her an extra degree of focus

during the afternoon class, and Ruth Garrick commented on it afterwards. 'That was a very nice session, Summer.'

'Yes, I think it's because they were all married couples, except Sally Clemson.'

'She's the mother of a newly diagnosed type one?'

'Yes. Bonnie Clemson is six, and that makes Mrs Clemson's involvement very strong, of course. Somehow today I really wanted to *prove* to them all that diabetes can actually strengthen their partnerships, not break them under the strain.'

Ruth nodded, her warm brown eyes inviting further details, although Summer didn't think that this was a conscious thing at all. She resisted the need to talk, though.

John and Alex really aren't my problem, unless John comes to me himself, she realised.

There was an hour to fill in before she was due to lead a support group meeting for type two diabetics and their families, but today there was no question of collating and stapling. She had plenty of reports and case notes to write up, and three phone calls to return to patients, wanting some simple advice.

Randall was about somewhere. She saw his coffee-cup on the draining-board in the kitchen, then went to the bathroom to find, when she came back, that it had gone and that his office door was now tightly closed. It seemed odd that she hadn't encountered him because his energetic presence was usually very apparent at the centre. Serious Steve tended to hide at times, absorbed in research and reading, but Randall never did.

Summer was due to meet Randall here straight after her support group meeting ended at seven, and she couldn't help a dark intuition, now, that the evening was going to be important.

He was waiting for her as promised when she emerged from the meeting-room shortly after seven, having chatted for a few extra minutes to the stragglers then tidied the room. In contrast to the afternoon class, the meeting had been rather fragmented and flat—with one elderly man determined to dwell at length on his golf game, despite all her attempts to keep the group's focus on concerns that were shared by the majority. So she felt tired and rather tense now.

Randall must have snatched the time to go home and shower as he was wearing fresh sand-coloured trousers and a white knit shirt that fell in loose, casual lines on his powerful frame. The ends of his dark hair were still slightly wet.

Summer had changed, too, before the support group, since she liked to create a slightly less formal impression during group meetings by wearing attractive street clothes rather than a uniform. But if Randall liked the apricot silk T-shirt-style blouse and navy linen-blend skirt he didn't comment.

'Hi. . .' He had turned at the sound of the meeting-room door closing and smiled when he saw her, but the smile was tight and automatic and quickly ebbed to leave a frown.

He looked badly on edge, causing her to say at once, 'If you have to cancel, that's fine. If something's come up. . .'

'No, I'm not cancelling.'

'Then what is it? What's the matter?'

'I hope it's nothing. I hope I've got it all wrong. We'll talk over dinner.' He moved restlessly away from her, making the loose shirt ripple across his firm torso. 'Let's lock up, shall we?'

'Everyone else has gone? Lesley? Steve?' She felt her nervousness increasing, evident now in dampened palms and heightened colour. This wasn't the way she wanted their first night together to begin!

'An hour ago,' he answered absently.

'Randall—?'

'Let's not hang around here.' Again he moved to put more distance between them and she began to feel quite sick.

It was then that both of them heard a car pull up in the street outside. A door banged, the vehicle drove off again and rapid, clattering feet sounded on the steps outside. Then came a desperate hammering on the door and the sound of a ragged, tearful voice.

'Dr Macleay? Sister Westholm? Dr Berg? Is anybody still there?'

It was Penny Malley, completely distraught.

'Sit down,' Summer urged after she'd unlocked the door quickly and pulled her inside. 'Drink some water. Or shall I make you some tea?'

'N-no.' Penny shook her head and dashed tears from her swollen eyes as a sob shook her once again. 'I d-don't—don't want. . .' She couldn't finish her sentence. She was pale and trembling, and when Summer touched her hand in a gesture of support she found it beaded with a cold, clammy sweat.

'What's happened, love?' she asked gently, although she knew already.

Randall had gone to the fridge in the corner of the room and was rummaging in the back of it. Summer frowned at him, angry. His ominous words to her a few moments ago, and now. . . Was he looking for his wretched coffee-cup again? It was right there on the draining-board! What *was* he doing? Surely the focus should be on Penny.

'Lar-Larry,' Penny began. She put a hand to her head and sat down, as if suddenly drained of her strength, and her trembling was far more pronounced.

'Randall?' Summer turned to him, her voice high. This wasn't just emotional upset. . .

Randall was already there, his search of the fridge

successful. 'Yes,' he said. 'Here's some orange juice. I think she's still in control enough to swallow it. Drink the juice, Penny,' he urged in a clear, authoritative tone. 'Stop trying to talk and just drink the juice!'

He tilted the narrow glass rim against her lips and she swallowed clumsily until the eight-ounce bottle was half-empty, then he took it away. In a remarkably short time the symptoms of hypoglycaemia began to disappear.

Meanwhile, Randall prepared some biscuits and peanut butter, as a supplemental, slowly digestible carbohydrate had to be given after the quick-acting glucose in the orange juice to maintain body glucose, restore liver glycogen and prevent secondary hypoglycaemia.

'You were quicker on the uptake than I was,' Summer murmured in a remorseful aside to him, forgetting their personal tensions for a moment.

'I saw how dilated her pupils were, and the way her nose and lips were blanched,' he murmured.

'I was too busy focusing on her emotional state and not on the symptoms of insulin reaction. I put the trembling and clammy hands down to feelings, not physiology.'

'You don't seem surprised that she's upset.'

'She was planning to tell Larry about her diabetes over dinner tonight.'

'Oh. . .and obviously it didn't go too well.'

They both turned to Penny, who took the biscuits and peanut butter and began to chew on them obediently but without enjoyment. Like most long-term diabetics, she was well schooled at eating when she wasn't hungry in order to maintain the correct balance between glucose and insulin.

'You told him?' Summer prompted unnecessarily.

'He couldn't take it at all,' Penny responded dully. 'He was so shocked—hadn't suspected—and I saw his face when I told him I'd have to inject four times a day for the rest of my life. You'd have thought I'd said I was a heroin addict. He'd heard about some of the complications of diabetes too. The worst ones, of course, like blindness, amputated feet. . .I told him that with good control, proper foot care and a sensible lifestyle—all of which I *have* now—I should be safe from any of that. We should even be able to have healthy, beautiful babies. But. . . He didn't say much. It was just his face. And I thought he'd take me in his arms and say it didn't matter!'

Randall prowled behind Penny's chair where the young diabetic woman couldn't see him. His teeth were clenched and he swore beneath his breath. Summer sat beside Penny, touching her arm and aching for her. The glow in her pretty brown eyes was extinguished, and her face—normally filled with energy and enthusiasm—was blotched and sagging.

And yet something in Penny's last words triggered a more thoughtful response in Summer, in contrast to the instinctive and generally justifiable anger which Randall always displayed when one of his patients was the victim of prejudice because of their disease.

'Hang on a minute, love,' she said to the young woman, just as the doctor left them for a moment to put the orange-juice bottle on the draining-board. 'Would you really have wanted him to say that straight away? In a way that's a superficial response. It sounds great but it might not hold up under pressure.'

'What do you mean?' Penny was listening very warily to this new idea.

Summer spoke slowly, gathering her thoughts as she voiced them. Randall had returned now and was listening in silence too. 'It's no use pretending that diabetes doesn't make a difference. It does. It takes courage to live with the disease, and some people don't have it. Diabetics *can't* walk away from it, though some of them try to.' She was thinking of John, as well as other patients she had known only professionally.

'I certainly used to a couple of years ago!' Penny agreed.

'But if you're not the one who's diabetic, if you're just a friend or a lover, then you have a choice.' Still Summer spoke very carefully. 'You *can* walk away, and there are some people who know it's the *only* thing they can do. Others—like Larry, perhaps—need to think, and once they've thought it through and decided that they *can* live with it the commitment they make is far bigger and stronger than if they'd promised undying love and support with their first breath.'

'Then you think—' Penny's face had brightened so much that Summer came in hastily again.

'Penny, I don't know. He may do that thinking and decide that he can't—that it's not fair to you or to himself to try—and if someone decides that then perhaps you have to respect it, tell yourself it's for the best. Just give him time. That's all I'm saying.'

Even as she said it she didn't know if it was the right advice. Some instinct told her, though, that this relationship could be saved as long as Penny didn't harden her heart against Larry's first reaction and find it impossible to forgive him later on if he did have a change of heart. . . Or was she just prolonging Penny's pain by giving her false hope?

Catching Randall's eye, she saw an icy hostility in his face that chilled her deeply. Clearly he didn't like what she had said. There was something else in his features too—something beyond anger, which she couldn't analyse now.

Trying to put aside all this, she lifted her chin and said in her most professional tone, 'But I think Dr Macleay has something to say as well.'

'Penny, you timed your insulin to cover a main meal

between seven and eight, didn't you?' the doctor asked woodenly. It wasn't the kind of thing Summer had meant, although—as before—she couldn't fault him for focusing primarily on Penny's physical well-being right now.

'Yes,' Penny nodded and sniffed. 'It's a chicken and almond casserole with avocado and artichoke salad and low-calorie chocolate mousse for dessert. It's all ready. But Larry's gone. . .'

'You'd better get back home, then, or you'll be late eating and that could throw you into another insulin reaction. Do you need a lift?'

'I came by taxi. I can ring for another one,' Penny said. 'It'll be the eating that's hard. I don't feel hungry at all.'

'Will you be alone in the house?'

'No, Mum and Dad should be home by now. I wanted the house to myself while I told Larry. That's why I planned it for a night when I knew they'd be late. I'd allowed for hors d'oeuvres, too, but we never ate them. I suppose that's why I had the reaction.' She wrung her hands distractedly.

'I'm going to drive you home,' Randall told her. 'Don't hang around waiting for a taxi.'

'OK, but I might just. . .use the bathroom.'

'Of course.' Penny ducked down the corridor and Randall turned to Summer. 'Will you lock up? Then perhaps you might as well head home. It's getting late.'

'Head home?' She tried to keep the tight, panicky note out of her voice. 'But—'

He met her bewildered look with blue eyes that both flamed and froze. 'I'm going to have to cancel our plans, I'm afraid. I'm. . .sorry.'

'I don't mind that it's a little later than expected, Randall,' she told him desperately. 'It's clear we have things to discuss.'

They both glanced down the corridor towards the bathroom but there was no sign of Penny yet, and in any case she was too involved in her own turmoil to be aware of the undercurrents of fraught meaning in what they had been saying to each other.

'Look,' he said very quietly, 'at the moment I don't think we do. I'm sorry. It seems clear to me now that it was a mistake for us to. . .embark on any sort of personal involvement. In fact, it probably should have been clear to me from the beginning so, if you like, I'll take the blame.'

'It's not a matter of taking blame, Randall,' she answered him wildly, only remembering to lower her voice when she caught his warning glare. 'I just feel. . .so completely in the dark, that's all. It's clear you disagree about what I've said to Penny.'

'This has very little to do with Penny.'

'Then—'

'Isn't it obvious? It's your response to John. Surely you know me well enough by now to realise what little sympathy I'd have for your feelings there?'

'Know you?' she echoed with a tight laugh. 'At the moment I wouldn't claim to know you at all, Randall Macleay.'

'Yes, well, the feeling's quite mutual, I assure you,' he muttered, then turned to Penny as she emerged from the bathroom. 'Let's go, shall we? You need to get home for dinner.'

CHAPTER EIGHT

'WHO else do we need to talk about this afternoon?' Randall asked, glancing down at some notes held in his left hand.

It was the diabetes care centre's semi-regular Monday afternoon conference, attended by Summer, Ruth Garrick, the two doctors and usually a couple of staff from the hospital as well. If Lesley Harper had management matters to discuss, as she did today, then time was left for this at the end of the meeting.

'Brian Page's mother rang,' Summer reported. 'She wants to come in and see you, Randall.' His name stuck in her throat a little. 'She's worried about him. I suggested she come to the support group meeting tonight as well.'

'Anything specific?' Randall asked, frowning as he glanced at her briefly. He had frowned a lot since last Wednesday evening's cryptic and painful confrontation. Summer wondered if it was obvious to the rest of the staff how deeply at odds they were, managing to maintain a superficial politeness only because what was wrong ran so very deep.

'Just what we're all aware of, I think—that he's still far too careless and defiant,' she said in her best professional tone. 'He had a major reaction, apparently.' She looked at the notes in her diary briefly. 'On the weekend, and if Mrs Page hadn't come home early from shopping he'd have passed out.'

'Does she want to bring Brian with her?'

'No. Really I think she just wants to talk and get some reassurance.'

'Sure. I wish there were some positive suggestions I could make, but there aren't. I've even thought about suggesting he try an insulin pump—'

'A pump? He'd have to be the worst candidate in the world for that!' Steve came in explosively.

'Well, yes.' Randall spread his hands. 'But there can be some value in setting someone a very high challenge like that.'

'But *Brian Page*?'

'No. You're right. I decided against it.'

'I should think so,' the more junior doctor exclaimed. 'It'd be laughable to try and get the right compliance from Brian Page.'

'But one patient who will be using the pump is Janey Gordon,' Randall said, and this was greeted appreciatively as Janey was popular with everyone.

'Yes, now she *is* an ideal candidate,' Dr Berg nodded.

'Glad you approve, Steve.' As usual he was needling the other doctor a little, but without the comic flair that normally made serious Steve enjoy it as much as everyone else. Summer wondered if everyone had noticed, as she had, that the candid humour she had loved in Randall seemed to have evaporated completely.

'Well, yes,' Steve said now, uneasy. 'I mean, I presume it's because she's planning to try a pregnancy.'

'Yes, but she may continue with the pump afterwards if she likes it. And there's no reason why she shouldn't be fertile. I've given the go-ahead for them to start trying in a few weeks, as soon as she's mastered the pump, so we may see her in here quite often over the next year or so, and I'll be working closely with Adam Snow, who'll be her obstetrician.'

'Good. I think we all hope it works out for her,' Lesley came in. 'Now, sorry to hurry things along but there's quite a bit to discuss on the issue of the annual fund-raising luncheon and garden party and Judy, you probably need to get back to the hospital.'

'Yes,' nodded the fourth-floor ward co-ordinator. 'I've been away longer than I said I would. We seemed to have a lot to get through today, and I'll have some phone calls to make about a couple of your patients when I get back.'

The matronly redhead left, Imelda joined the group and Lesley took the floor.

'Now, I've negotiated successfully with Vincent Giangrande,' she said. 'He and his family are happy to let us use Olivewood House for the occasion. . .'

Randall's brief glance again. Summer stared down. She had known that Lesley was trying to get a new location for the fund-raiser this year, but hadn't known until now who the place belonged to.

And what did that look of Randall's mean? She wanted to confront him again, to insist that they talk, but just how much humiliation was she prepared to risk? Perhaps all that had happened, at the heart of the matter, was that he had changed his mind about what he felt and was uncomfortable and regretful that he'd compromised the ease of their professional relationship by forming a personal one in the first place. In fact, he had said something very close to that on that difficult night.

'It's a magnificent house with gorgeous grounds,' the centre's manager enthused. 'A masterpiece of twentieth-century design. Used to belong to a best-selling thriller novelist and many of the art-deco pieces he had collected were sold with the house.'

'It sounds great, Lesley,' Steve said, blinking behind his wire-framed glasses. 'I'm looking forward to seeing it myself. What made them decide to be so generous?'

'Well, Maya Giangrande has been one of our patients for a long time, of course, and now there's John as well. They're a wealthy family and I think the house is underused at the moment, with just Mr Giangrande and his wife in residence.'

'Good timing for us, then.'

'It is.'

She went on to talk about the rest of the plans for the fund-raiser but Summer couldn't concentrate, aware that Randall was still watching her.

It's because Lesley's been talking about the Giangrandes, she realised. He talked about John the other night. Does he think I want him back? That I've been regretting my forfeited chance at wealth, or something?

John had been in to see Randall on Friday and had been closeted in his office for some time. Emerging, he had seen Summer and acknowledged her absently. He had looked miserably down and if he had given her the slightest encouragement she would have tried to get him to talk, but he hadn't—just reported briefly, 'Going to try the jet injector.' Although her heart had twisted at how much of a struggle this all was for him there had also been a deep sense within her that he was quite a stranger. Not someone she had ever known, or ever could know, with true intimacy and understanding.

If there's any help I can give him then the first move has to come from him, she had decided again.

'So, if anybody *dares* to make any other plans for Friday the fourteenth or Saturday the fifteenth of August, I'll personally make your life miserable,' Lesley finished.

Her fiercely efficient glare swept over the group of four, coming to rest—with emphasis, it seemed—on Summer. The latter flushed guiltily. No, she *hadn't* been listening. Had Lesley guessed? Fortunately, her attention had focused again just in time to hear those all-important dates.

'The fourteenth and the fifteenth,' she repeated dutifully, scribbling them down and trying to seem organised—which, actually, she normally was. This was

Randall's problem, not hers! she decided, wanting to be angry with him since anger was sometimes easier to bear than pain.

'But won't the Ladies' Hospital Auxiliary do the setting-up on the Friday?' Steve asked.

'Yes, but it scarcely looks good if we don't turn up to help.' Lesley frowned at him. 'Summer, will you have a class that Friday?'

'Um. . .' She flipped through her work-diary hastily. 'No, I've got nothing more now until the third of September.'

'Good, then we can actually close the centre at lunch-time that day and all spend the afternoon at Olivewood.'

'I'll pencil it in,' Steve murmured.

'*Ink* it in, Dr Berg!' Lesley insisted.

'Don't you have this sort of thing in the United States?' Summer asked him.

'Well, yes, but it's not quite the same. This is kind of like girl scouts. Jolly good show, everyone pitching in, doing our bit folding table napkins, tally-ho,' he mimicked, in an execrable plum-in-the-mouth accent.

Randall roused himself enough to chuckle. 'Girl scouts, are we? That's a new way of looking at it.'

'I think you'd find it hard to get a uniform that fitted, Randall,' Lesley teased, but he only grunted and gave a token half-smile, before subsiding with a scowl into the depths of his swivel chair.

A few minutes later the meeting was over.

'I'll lock up,' Summer offered. 'I'll be back this evening for the type one support group.'

'That's right.' Lesley nodded. 'I'd forgotten that was tonight. Did I buy enough milk and biscuits this morning?'

'Not quite, but I'll pick up some supplies over dinner,' Summer said. 'Don't worry. I wasn't planning to go home before the group so I've got plenty of time.'

She left the office and went into the meeting-room to check that it was in order for the evening. It wasn't, quite. The cleaner had stacked the chairs against the wall so she arranged them in a circle. About twelve people usually came to the group, which met once a fortnight.

Like the type two group, it was open to close family members as well as diabetics themselves and Summer found the sessions very satisfying as they could spend longer on the sorts of issues and feelings that couldn't be fitted into a regular doctor's appointment at the centre.

After arranging the room, she went out to snatch a quick meal and buy the necessary milk and biscuits. By ten to seven she was back, putting the kettle on to boil for tea and spooning coffee into the cone-shaped paper filter of the electric coffee-maker.

Someone was early. She heard footsteps outside, first walking up to the front door and then pausing as if in uncertainty before making their way round to the side. The sound told Summer that it must be someone new as group regulars knew that it was the side door leading directly into the meeting-room that was opened for evening sessions. Pausing for a moment to switch on the coffee-maker, Summer then went through to the side door to make the newcomer feel welcome.

It was a thin, dark and rather good-looking young man who stood there on the step, shifting a little nervously from foot to foot, and Summer didn't recognise him at all. Not a patient, certainly, and too young to be one of the parents of diabetic children. Perhaps he was lost and just wanted directions up to the hospital car park.

'Can I help you?' she asked politely.

'Um. . . Is there a meeting here tonight? For diabetics and people who want to know about it?'

'Yes, that's right. Are you meeting someone here?'

'Well, I was hoping I could join in. I—I'm not diabetic myself but I have a, well, a friend who is.'

'A friend?'

'Yes, Penny Malley. Do you know her?'

'Yes, I do. I like Penny a lot.'

'My name is Larry Bowden.'

Larry! Biting back a dozen things she could have said, wanted to say and definitely *shouldn't* say, Summer *did* say carefully, 'Of course. Penny's mentioned you. Yes, you're very welcome to join in. We usually have mainly diabetics themselves or their spouses. Occasionally a parent or a child, but I can understand that as a close friend you have lots of questions.'

'Oh, not lots,' he hedged. 'I don't want to hog the limelight or anything. I'd just like to listen.'

'Well, that's fine, too, but please don't feel afraid to speak if something comes up. You're a bit early, actually. People start drifting in at about seven and we make tea and coffee and don't usually sit down till about a quarter past—so if there's anything you'd like to talk about just to me now. . .'

'No, it's OK, thanks.'

'Some tea or coffee, then?'

'Tea, please.'

'Come through and make it yourself, then it'll be just how you like it. There are biscuits as well.'

He nodded and followed her in silence, and once again she had to resist the urge to speak, wanting to prompt him and try to draw him out—wanting most of all to ask about Penny and if he had seen her since he had fled her house last Wednesday. It was an awkward few minutes as they waited for others to arrive. Larry mooched about the meeting-room, sipping his tea and reading the diabetes-related posters on the walls.

About fifteen minutes later, after greetings and conversation, the group gathered and discussion began. It was a small turn-out tonight as the fine evening had tempted people out of doors. Brian Page's mother had come, as Summer had suggested, and an older married couple of whom the wife was insulin-dependent and the husband able to control his disease through oral hypoglycaemics. Two more women, one married and one single, had each come alone.

'I just don't know what to do about Brian,' was Mrs Page's predictable opening, and for half an hour people tossed anecdotes around and tried to come up with helpful suggestions. Summer directed the flow of talk a little, but was content to stay in the background. Larry didn't say anything at all.

The most helpful idea came from Caroline Sedgewick, the unmarried woman, who was in her early thirties. 'Perhaps the problem isn't his diabetes at all,' she said. 'After all, plenty of teenagers who aren't diabetic have problems. Could it be boredom, or uncertainty about a career, or unhappiness over a girl? Perhaps if there *was* some other thing and it could be resolved then his attitude to diabetes would improve as a result. I know that was the case with me in my teens.'

'Tell us more about it, Caroline,' Summer prompted.

'Well, my parents always encouraged me to stay close to home and not get very committed to outside interests. They thought that dealing with my insulin doses and so on was enough of a commitment, but of course it wasn't.'

'And what changed that for you?'

'Painting. It was only when I took that up, and started trekking about all over the islands, that I found a focus and had an incentive to keep my diabetes under control and at the same time not to get destructively obsessed with it, as I had been before.'

'Yes, yes,' Mrs Page said, her face brightening as the

other woman spoke. 'It's true that Brian is very uncertain about what he wants to do as a career. My husband and I have been telling him, and telling each other, that once he is dealing with his diabetes better then it'll be time to start thinking seriously about his future, but perhaps it's the other way around.'

She didn't say much more after this but Summer could see her thinking, her face at times serious and at times far more relaxed than Summer had seen it during their two previous encounters. Meanwhile, the discussion had become more general and very wide-ranging.

Sometimes Summer set up a rough agenda, or a topic to focus on for the evening, but in a small group like this one she felt that she didn't need to and that people would naturally gravitate to the things that were on their minds. Tonight it was everything from new recipes to who to tell about the disease and when.

'I told my office manager, but not the big boss,' Caroline said. 'He's an ogre and wouldn't be any help if I had a reaction anyway. Whereas my office manager is really nice and knows exactly where to find the glucose lozenges in my purse.'

'I tell as many people as possible,' Mrs Oakley said. 'With Mike out at work all day, I don't always feel safe since I'm one of those people who find it very difficult to feel a reaction coming on.'

'Not that you've had one for several months, love,' her husband said.

Summer found that her mind was wandering. She wasn't really needed tonight as the group was small enough to direct itself, and discussion was flowing nicely. Larry had clearly made up his mind that he didn't want to talk, and she didn't dare risk putting him off by pestering. She wondered whether Randall would approve of how she was handling Larry's presence.

Will I tell him? I suppose I'll have to. . .

The group was looking expectantly at her, and after a covert glance at her watch Summer realised that it was almost fifteen minutes beyond their usual finishing time. 'Yes, we'll stop now, shall we?' she came in, guiltily aware that her focus had been less than usual tonight and less than it should have been.

'Are tickets to the fund-raising luncheon available yet?' Mr Oakley wanted to know.

'Not yet. By Friday, I think. It's another two weeks away.'

'Will you be going, Sister Westholm?'

'Of course, and to the garden party, but more as a helper than a guest,' she answered.

'We'll see you there, then, if not before.'

'Yes, in my new dress!'

'And Angela? It'd be nice to catch up with her again.' Having been associated with the centre since their marriage and arrival in Bermuda two years ago, the Oakleys knew Summer's predecessor quite well.

'I think she's going. I'm not sure,' Summer said. 'She's feeling the heat with her pregnancy, apparently.'

'And what about you. . .er. . . Larry?' Caroline Sedgewick asked. The group must have been curious about the silent newcomer tonight, but each had hidden it well.

'What luncheon is this?' he asked, clearly reluctant to have the focus on him, no matter how casually.

'It's the diabetes care centre's annual fund-raiser on the fifteeth of August,' Summer came in quickly. 'There's a formal luncheon, and then a garden party afterwards. This year it's being held at Olivewood House in Tucker's Town. The luncheon is quite expensive, of course, but the garden party should be fun, and that's only ten dollars per person and it includes a Devonshire tea.'

'Do come!' Mrs Page said. 'It's a good way to meet

people on the islands.' Clearly, she assumed that he was a shy newcomer to Bermuda, and neither Larry himself nor Summer chose to correct her.

'I'll see if I'm free,' he said awkwardly, then took car keys from his pocket and jiggled them nervously, before saying a quick general goodnight and ducking out the side door in the wake of Mr and Mrs Oakley.

Summer almost called him back, but then his name died on her lips. What would she say? She didn't know if the discussion tonight had helped him at all. Indeed, she could only guess at the help he needed.

'Surely this means he's decided he *can* make a commitment to Penny,' she said to Randall the next morning.

'Or perhaps he wants to prove to himself that he's made the right decision already,' the doctor growled. 'That diabetics have far too many problems for him to take on.'

The hostile rebuff made her so miserable that she simply turned away, not caring if he saw her pain. With numb hands she gathered up her work-diary and notes, ready to head up to the hospital—not aware that Randall was still there, watching her, until she heard his voice, slightly scratchy, saying her name.

'Summer?'

'Yes, Randall?' It took an immense effort to have to face him, and when she did she knew that her face was tight and pale.

He hesitated for a tautly stretched second, then said, 'Nothing. I— Let's just hope you're right about Larry, that's all.'

It was the closest they had come to any sort of softening since last Wednesday, and it wasn't much so she only nodded and got herself away.

CHAPTER NINE

IN THE days that followed there was no word or sign from either Penny or Larry.

Since Penny's blood sugar was now well controlled on the new regime of more injections and closer self-monitoring there was no reason to expect frequent calls from her and no need to set up appointments to see her beyond regular check-ups, so the fact that she didn't put in an appearance wouldn't normally be cause for concern.

And as for Larry... He'd said nothing that night at the support group meeting so why should Summer hope that he'd been interested enough to come again? It began to look as if Randall's assessment was the correct one—all the support group meeting had done was confirm Larry's fear that it was too much to handle.

Meanwhile, with all the other patients on file at the centre, it wasn't something that anyone could afford to dwell on. The fund-raising lunch at Olivewood House was rapidly approaching too. Lesley was by turns elated and dramatically in despair over the arrangements, proclaiming one day, 'If I'm always looking at the ground these days, everyone, it's only to try and avoid all the *toes* I'm in danger of treading on!'

And speaking of avoidance... It was becoming a pattern between Randall and Summer, and she was sure that the other staff must have noticed it too. They were both almost too careful to apologise if ever they accidentally touched each other.

He acts as if he's burnt me or something. And, of course, the funny thing is—that's the way it feels. His touch seemed to stay on her skin for minutes afterwards, and the warm, musky scent of him seemed to linger in her nostrils. When their eyes met they both flinched away, and if ever they laughed at the same time the sound quickly dried up.

All she could be glad of was that they had chosen to keep quiet about all those sailing expeditions a few weeks ago, which meant that at least there were no awkward questions about their relationship from the other staff. Just some odd glances from Lesley sometimes, and perhaps Imelda's wide smile came less often than it usually did, extinguished by a nameless change in Randall, whose personality was so close to the heart of the centre's pleasant atmosphere.

The confident, wickedly humorous man Summer thought she knew, and knew she loved, had gone, it seemed—to be replaced by an efficient figure who got the job done with as much dedication as ever but with none of the flair. She wasn't the only one to notice the fact.

'Funny,' mused serious Steve, rumpling his blond hair and speaking half to himself one Wednesday morning in the little kitchen when the fund-raiser at Olivewood House was just three days away. 'I understand him better these days, but I like him less.'

Hard on the heels of this observation, Randall himself appeared, studied the draining-board and counter-top grimly for a minute, reached into the cupboard above the sink to extract his blue mug, then poured himself a coffee and disappeared again, muttering, 'Why she can't do I ask and leave it in plain view. . .?

'Let's amend that,' Steve said. 'I understand his *conversation* better. *Him* I don't understand at all!'

Summer flushed and murmured something unintelligible. Clearly Steve didn't have any notion that the change might have anything to do with her. Indeed, she was beginning to wonder about it herself. Maybe there was something else going on in his life that she knew nothing about. It was all a painful and ongoing mystery, but she had too much pride to try and solve it by direct questioning. It would be too humiliating to probe, only to discover that his interest had simply evaporated.

She remembered that he was divorced. His marriage had been an immature mistake long ago, he had said, but perhaps he was the kind of man who lost interest very suddenly when things reached a certain level of depth.

No, surely not!

'I'm telling you, avoid Lesley like the plague for at least the next hour, girl,' Imelda warned, coming into the kitchen to get coffee for herself.

Steve had gone, as had Randall, but Summer was still dithering, watching the coffee-machine as it finished its dripping and on the point of deciding against coffee at all.

At her questioning look Imelda explained, 'There's been a nice mix-up about the chairs for Saturday. Not my fault, thank the Lord! Do you have hospital patients to see this morning?'

'Yes, in fifteen minutes.'

'You're lucky!'

Lesley was, indeed, still fuming and wailing about the chairs when Summer left ten minutes later, but she found this infinitely easier to shrug off than Randall's far more circumspect emotions earlier, and enjoyed her session with the two patients she had come to see.

First there was Anne Crossland, a type one diabetic who was pregnant with her second child and hospitalised due to persistent pre-term labour that was not directly related to her diabetes. Summer was making a weekly visit to her to help with her foot-care routine and advise Anne and the staff in the obstetrics wing on any problems or questions that might arise beyond the province of Randall's close surveillance.

Today Summer gave extra attention to a ridge of calloused tissue on Mrs Crossland's left heel that was looking a little inflamed, soaking it for a few minutes then using a buffing pad, but she was confident that it wouldn't get out of control.

'And you were going to give me Janey Gordon's phone number,' the patient reminded Summer now.

'That's right. Thanks so much for volunteering to talk to her.'

'Well, this is my second pregnancy, and I used an insulin pump for the first one, too, so I feel like quite an expert. No offence to you medical people, but there are details that only another diabetic can really understand and I'd have done better with my first pregnancy if I'd had someone who'd already been through it to help me.'

'I think she'll really appreciate it. And I'm sure the two of you will get on well.'

'Oh, yes! We've met up in the waiting-room at the centre once or twice and had a nice chat, but each time one of us has been called in for her appointment before we got around to exchanging phone numbers.'

'Let me know how it goes when I see you next week.'

'I will.'

Next there was Ray Lewis. He was a type two diabetic who was in for an unrelated and minor heart procedure. Randall had been supervising his insulin therapy so she had little to do for him but could spare five minutes to check that he had no specific problems.

He didn't, but when she ran her eye briefly over his chart he asked, 'Does it have my weight down there? I've lost four kilograms in the past month, Sister Westholm. Aren't you pleased?'

And she was—because this was another moderate and

well-controlled drop, and he was well on the way to shedding the weight that had contributed to the onset of his disease and would exacerbate it if he was careless about diet.

'And it's all been through sensible eating, as I learnt in your classes,' Mr Lewis added.

'You're doing really well!'

When she returned to the centre Lesley had forgotten about the chairs. Penny Malley and Larry Bowden had turned up, and it was immediately clear that everything was going to be all right.

'We're both taking the day off work,' Penny confessed. 'But I don't think my boss will mind. I haven't exactly been selling a lot of Irish linen over the past couple of weeks. You were right, Sister Westholm, he just needed the time.'

From the corner of her eye Summer could see Lesley, hovering curiously at the door of her office, ostensibly on a phone call, and Imelda was quite openly eavesdropping, and beaming from ear to ear, too, which was a welcome sight these days.

'It was just something I'd never thought about,' Larry said, looking a little awkward but very happy. 'Penny was right to be angry at my first reaction. . . Thank goodness she got over that!'

'Thank goodness *you* did, Larry.'

'I've still got a lot of questions,' he said now, frowning. 'Like, would it be possible to get Penny to have an insulin reaction some time in controlled conditions so I'd know what to look for if it happened for real?'

'Oh, that's not necessary,' Summer answered. 'Penny's mother has seen her reactions before, and she is very experienced in dealing with them so she can explain the symptoms to you.'

Larry nodded in agreement. 'I'm a motor mechanic,

see,' Larry explained seriously. 'I can kind of relate to an illness like this. It's like fine-tuning the fuel and the engine. I feel like it's an illness you can win over, if you're careful. It's *predictable*. I like that. There were a couple of books from the library—'

'He's been reading like mad, apparently,' Penny came in. 'And then last night he just turned up at my front door and—'

'I'm OK when I *understand* something,' Larry said.

'Is Dr Macleay around? We'd like to tell him, too.'

'Tell him what?' Randall said, appearing at the door of the waiting-room.

'That we're getting married,' Penny announced, her face glowing and alive.

'Wow! Congratulations!'

'Not for a year. But you'll all be invited. You've done so much! And thank you, Summer, for what you said three weeks ago.'

'Oh, it was nothing,' she muttered.

Randall was looking at her, and she didn't want to see what was written on his face. It was great about Penny and Larry and it was nice to have her controversial advice to Penny vindicated, but if Randall was tempted to apologise... That would do so little to mend what was really wrong that she'd probably laugh in his face.

Or cry, maybe. Crying was a distinct temptation at times, but she hadn't given in to it *yet*.

Penny and Larry left a few minutes later, to have a lobster lunch at a fancy restaurant, and Randall went up to the hospital to see a thyroid patient just out of surgery. When he was safely gone and the coast was clear Summer set off for her usual short lunch break in the botanical gardens, taking a chance on the rain that threatened in the form of splendid clouds massing in the sky beyond Hamilton.

But the coast turned out not to be clear after all. She was seen, just as she crossed Point Finger Road, though she didn't notice the dark-haired figure who was closing in on her from behind until he hailed her just as she entered the lush reaches of the gardens.

'Summer! Summer, wait!'

John.

She turned. 'Goodness, you startled me!'

'Sorry.' He looked down at her packet of sandwiches, piece of fruit and bottle of mineral water. 'Lunch? You don't think it's going to rain?'

'Probably,' she conceded. 'But I'm playing chicken with that big black cloud right over there. How are you, John?'

'Oh, good. . .good. Let's walk.'

'Sure. You've got an appointment?'

'Yes, but I'm early. Hey, here's a statistic I'm quite proud of. I've been testing my blood glucose *religiously* four times a day for the past week and a half, and haven't had a single reading outside the desirable range.'

'Really? That's great! Be sure to tell Dr Macleay, won't you?'

'What do you think? It's half the reason I wanted to see him. Doing well with my new jet injector, too.'

She took out a sandwich and ate it as they strolled, taking the walkway which led down to the groupings of huge fig trees whose aerial root systems had reached to the ground to create massive, complex formations of limbs—like some primal natural sculpture. They didn't talk much, just exchanged bits of safe news. Summer's father had resurfaced in England again, apparently, safe and sound and satisfied. John's mother had been away too, visiting her sister in Boston, but was now immersed in readying Olivewood House for Saturday.

Yes, all very safe, but Summer was left with a sense of new maturity and determination in John. Those blood-sugar readings were excellent and no exaggeration, either, as his new and nifty little state-of-the-art meter had a memory which could store and display several thousand items of information in a wide variety of formats, so she'd seen the data for herself.

And then it *did* rain, the clouds opening with typical abruptness and the curtain-like downpour chasing in their wake back up the hill. Randall saw them as he hurried towards the centre, too, a newspaper held protectively over his head. Summer was laughing at that moment since she had begun to find these Bermuda rainstorms exhilarating as she got used to them, and this time they'd managed to stay ahead of the worst of it. John was slightly behind her, as he'd had to stop to put his meter inside his light suit jacket for protection.

'Hey!' he was calling. '*You've* probably got a spare uniform, but *I* have an important business meeting after this and no spare suit handy!'

Randall reached the shelter of the centre's front veranda first and stood waiting for them, his face impassive. As Summer reached the shelter too she felt like a schoolgirl late for class under that unreadable scrutiny.

Randall looked at his watch. 'I can see you straight away, John, if you'd like.'

'Thanks, yes. I do need to prepare for my meeting *and* dry out a little.'

'Come through, then.'

Summer was left to follow in their wake, but was then called in to Randall's consulting-room almost immediately. Closing the door, she realised that it was the first time they'd been alone together like this—an odd, awkward little triangle of people who each had a double relationship with each other, professional and personal.

'I realised we haven't checked the circulation in John's feet since he's been coming here,' Randall said, his tone medical and stiff. 'And he says it wasn't done up at the hospital, either. It's probably about time we did that.'

'Yes, although initially in London you did learn about foot care, didn't you, John?'

'Not sure if I took it all in back then,' he admitted. 'But lately I've been pretty good about checking for problems and I haven't noticed any. If my blood sugar isn't high then I'm unlikely to develop problems, aren't I, Dr Macleay?' He was clearly eager for a positive answer, and seemed quite oblivious to any tension between his doctor and his former fiancée.

All he's thinking about is himself and his illness, Summer realised. Which is how it should be in this situation. I'm the one who's reacting badly here. I *hate* this!

'Yes, but all the same,' Randall was saying, 'we should check. Could you handle it, Summer, while I look over all the data stored on this wondrous little meter he's brought in for me?'

But the humour was all on the surface.

Summer checked the pulse in each of John's feet and noted their temperature and colour, all of which were good. Then she tested his reflexes and checked his ability to feel vibrations in the foot, as well as his perception of the touch of sharp and dull objects.

'Can you feel the pen, John? What's it doing?'

'Scratching my instep.'

'And now?'

'Scratching the ball of my foot.'

'And. . .?'

'Rolling against my heel. . . My outer instep. . . My little toe.'

'It all seems fine, Dr Macleay,' she reported.

He had been fiddling with the meter, and copying a few figures from it into John's file. Now he looked up and nodded briefly, then she saw the sudden sharp focus of his blue eyes on her left hand and realised that she was still resting it on John's propped-up foot. It hadn't been an intimate gesture at all, and it was over now as John was reaching down to put socks and shoes back on. But Randall's piercing regard made it seem and feel intimate, and she felt the heat rise in her face and lost the ability to return his gaze.

'It all seems fine,' she repeated. 'The pulse was strong and both feet good and warm. Um, was that all you wanted me for?'

'Yes. Thanks. It bought me the time I needed to successfully disguise the fact that I hadn't encountered this precise species of gadget before,' he answered lightly. 'Did you get this in the US, John?'

'Yes, it's only been out for about six months, I think.'

'They're improving these meters all the time,' Randall agreed. 'This is virtually a computer. It's pretty impressive.'

'I was in New York ten days ago and picked it up then. Not cheap, of course.'

'These things never are when they're new.'

John shrugged. 'Well, that's what you're paying for—to have the best available, and to have it first. I expect I'll go on upgrading each time something new comes out. You don't keep abreast of all this yourself?'

Summer recognised the questions more as an example of John's innate, youthful arrogance about his wealth than a dig against Randall, but the latter had stiffened although he concealed it so well that she didn't think John had noticed.

'I read about everything that comes out, of course,' Randall said evenly. 'But if I ordered in samples it would bankrupt me fairly quickly, wouldn't it? As you say, some of these things are very expensive. And there aren't many patients in this practice who want to keep changing their system every time there's something new. Your Aunt Maya, for example, likes to stick very much to what she knows.'

'True,' John agreed easily. 'Well, I'm happy to show you my latest toy each time I do upgrade.'

'Thanks. I'll remember the offer. Now, did you want to talk privately. . .?'

Summer recognised her cue and left, very relieved to be out of that atmosphere. She didn't see John after his appointment had ended as she was busy in one of the small examining rooms, taking routine observations on a patient who would then be seeing Steve, and it wasn't until the end of the day that she had more than a snatched moment with Randall either.

The centre had quietened down by this time. Ruth had been in for some individual counselling sessions on diet and meal-planning that afternoon, but had just left. Imelda was tidying her desk. Lesley was hot on the trail of some chairs, and Steve had a patient to see up at the hospital.

Summer went into the little kitchen, saw that it was a mess and began to rinse cups and wipe down bench-tops.

'I'll get to it in a minute, girl, don't you worry,' Imelda called out, but Summer really didn't mind and had said so before Randall made his appearance, at which point she *did* mind, after all, and would have loved to slink away but it was too late.

'I haven't had a chance to apologise yet,' he said to her straight away.

'For what?' The kitchen was too small. It was . . .*unfair* that she had to stand close to him like this, able to feel his warmth and the gravitational pull of his bulk on her slighter form. 'Here, pass me your mug,' she ordered, in an attempt to make this horrible melting feeling go away.

'No, I'll do it.'

They eyed each other. Summer was in the way. Randall couldn't reach the sink. She stepped back and he passed her, clearing his throat and just weighing the mug in his hand—making no attempt either to rinse it or put it down.

'For criticising your advice to Penny about Larry three weeks ago,' he said. 'Obviously you were right and I was wrong.'

'Which sounds like an accusation when you say it in that tone,' she returned, deeply uneasy.

'Does it?'

'Yes!'

'Then I should apologise again.'

'No, don't,' she came in hastily, having no desire to prolong this. 'I know you're happy about Penny and Larry. We all are. And I'm not going to take any credit for it. When something's very strong between two people it wins out, regardless of good advice or the lack of it.'

'Do you think so?'

'Yes. Don't you?'

'Not necessarily. Which brings me to my next point.' He paused and cleared his throat again, making Summer look up, startled, from her wistful inspection of a juicy-looking thumbnail. She hid the thumbnail inside her fist very firmly. It was an awful habit, and Randall Macleay was *not* going to drive her to it!

His apology about Penny and Larry had been only the appetiser, she now saw. *This* was the main course.

'Yes, Randall?' she managed.

'John came to see me for a talk today, as you know.'

'Yes. . .?' It was unlike him to be so lacking in fluency.

Behind them his awkward pause was punctuated by Imelda's departure as she carefully closed the front door.

'Hell!' he said, and then it came flooding out in a rapid, angry flow, like that of a river bursting with storm water. 'He wants to try an insulin pump now. I told him he wasn't ready for it, asked him why he was so keen to try it. Sure it offers perhaps *the* best chance at full control, but it requires a hell of a lot of commitment, knowledge and discipline. You know that as well as I do. . . And do you know what he said?'

'Wh-what?'

'I'm quoting, Summer.' It was a threat. 'I'm quoting! "It's the only way I'll feel I have a chance of getting back the woman I love." What the hell do you want from the man?' His eyes blazed painfully, and she was so horrified at his words that she was speechless.

'You, of all people,' he went on. 'Someone who's in a unique position to be the best possible wife for a diabetic man. As his doctor, I have to ask you to try again—try to get over your fears. As your colleague, yes, I understand that your deeper knowledge of the issues might make it harder to commit yourself, but surely if you really care. . . Then, though,' he laughed harshly, 'as a man who was aching—who's still aching, though at times I hate myself for it—to become your lover, I keep telling myself why try to convince you? His loss would be my gain. I should just carry you into my bed as I so nearly did three and a half weeks ago and forget about John, except that I can't because I can't—*possibly*—love a woman who'd reject a man because of his diabetes!'

'This is about John's *diabetes*?' she whispered hoarsely at last, scarcely registering the full implication of everything he had said.

'Yes, of course it is!' He looked at her and she could see in his face just how much he despised what he thought was her attitude.

But there was something else, too—the unmistakable pull of desire and a deep connection that went beyond even that. Overpowered by it, she was as angry as he was now.

'His diabetes has *never* been an issue, Randall, and the fact that you could believe—and still do believe—that it is. . .I can't believe you've been putting me through all this because you could believe *that* of me!'

She moved convulsively to pass him, suddenly tear-blinded, and cannoned into him as he came forward to stop her. There was one tiny moment in which she had time to feel that pull again—a primitive, total response that encompassed his warm male scent in her nostrils, his densely healthy bulk and the intangible aura of his personality—and then there was a hiss of breath from his lips, followed by a high-pitched crash, and they both looked down to see his blue mug smashed to smithereens all over the floor.

'Oh, God, I'm sorry, Randall, I—'

'Do you think I care about that?'

He tried to seize her, but she shook herself free and bent down. The shards of china crunched beneath her feet and she took a paper towel and started to try to sweep them into a pile.

'Stop it! You'll cut yourself. Forget about it, anyway. We need to talk.'

'We don't!' She straightened and met his gaze. 'You've said enough already. I—I just need to go.'

'To John.'

'No, not to John. John is really quite irrelevant, actually!'

'Is he? Is he really? As his doctor— Hell, I wish at the moment that I wasn't his doctor!'

'I know. So do I. But you are, and it's beginning to look like we'll never get past that, doesn't it?'

He gave a brief, silent nod, and closed his eyes.

This time, when she made to leave, he didn't try to stop her. Gathering her things, she let herself out and paused at the door just long enough to hear the sound of him still in the kitchen, sweeping up the broken china. It was only much later that night that it finally occurred to her. In amongst that long, angry tirade he'd said that he loved her.

CHAPTER TEN

'HE BROKE it? Oh, no! How?' Imelda was saying to Lesley as Summer entered the diabetes care centre the next morning.

'Just let it slip while he was rinsing it out, he said—just after you'd gone. Steve came back from the hospital in time to see the last of the pieces going into the bin. He said there were thousands of them.'

'Well, it was a big mug. He'll be going round like a bear with a sore head!'

'He is! At least,' Lesley amended with a doubtful frown, 'he's certainly in a state.'

'Summer, did you hear what Lesley said?'

'Yes! How awful!'

She carefully pushed the new china mug she had bought last night further down into her bag. If Randall had taken the blame upon himself and said that he'd been alone then she couldn't let anyone find out that she had known about the mug in time to buy him this replacement last night, straight after leaving. Clearly, he didn't want anyone to suspect that there had been a scene, and on that issue she was in full agreement.

The replacement wasn't perfect, anyway. In her keyed-up state last night it had seemed crazy at first to catch a bus into Hamilton for the last half-hour of shopping, then to desperately scour the stores for a replica of that unique blue thing, but somehow it had helped.

It had helped later, too, as that realisation kept drumming in her head. He said he loved me. Something concrete to cling to, perhaps, when she wasn't in a mood to believe that love, under the current circumstances, could possibly be enough.

In the end she'd come close to a match for the shattered original. It was big, thick and bowl-shaped, with a sturdy handle well suited to dangling from a finger, but it wasn't quite the same shape and it wasn't blue, and she could only hope that a light, turquoise-tinted sea-green would do as well.

Buying a gift for him when she was badly angry, hurt and confused had felt odd, yet good in the end. She was less angry now. Drained, actually, in the aftermath of a bad night's sleep, not sure how they would manage to deal with each other from now on, or if anything could be salvaged out of all the promise that had existed so recently between them. He said he loved me, but. . .

Why had he been so ready to doubt her motives for breaking her engagement to John? That was the thing she found hardest to get past. Surely there should have been more trust, more faith in her integrity! It wasn't just her advice to Penny Malley that had made him doubt her. What was it, and when had it begun? That morning when they had had breakfast on Pebble Island and he'd asked her about John and their broken engagement?

So the mug helped, but she hid it in her bag and would have to pretend this afternoon, when she showed the others before she presented it to him, that she had bought it after lunch.

As it was Thursday, there were no appointments at the centre in the afternoon and Summer had time off. She used it most prosaically to do her grocery shopping and then returned to the centre just before five for evening hours, able to present the mug now.

Everyone was there except Randall himself, who was still at his outpatient clinic at the hospital. Imelda and Lesley had been busy with preparations for Saturday, Ruth had had a cooking class and Steve had just returned from golf, but when Summer pulled out her tissue-wrapped mug. . .

'Oh! Unbelievable!' Steve said. 'I got him one too!'

'So did I,' Lesley came in, and then Imelda and Ruth both burst out laughing and brought out their own contributions.

They were all still laughing when Randall walked in, to be greeted by the sight of five variations on the theme of blue china drinking vessels grouped on the desk in the middle of the open-plan office.

'What in the world. . .'

'Obviously we were *all* individually terrified that you'd fall apart without one,' Lesley said. 'There was no collusion here, Randall, I assure you! This accounts for why everyone has been mysteriously absent on errands at some point during the day.'

Each of the mugs was different. Imelda had got the colour right, but hers was far too small and the handle was hopeless for dangling. Steve's was big but it was too square, quite the wrong shade of blue and had a most distracting geometric pattern. Lesley had the colour fairly close, but the tall, elegantly shaped piece of bone china didn't remotely approximate the utilitarian mood of the original article. Ruth's attempt was simply a pretty blue mug with a picture of some birds and flowers on it.

And then there was Summer's, standing out from the group because it wasn't blue.

Randall was laughing now too. 'I'm sorry you all seem to think my sanity is so fragile! Should I accept all of them, and drink out of each one in turn?'

'They're all nice mugs,' Steve suggested. 'Why don't you choose your favourite and then we'll each keep our own contribution. I know the one I've been using has been chipped for months.'

'That sounds like a good plan. And you're all going to watch me doing it, aren't you?'

'Of course,' said Lesley, 'although, now that they're all together I can see *immediately* which one you'll pick.' She flashed a quick, probing glance at Summer. 'It's clear which one of us knows and understands you best.'

Summer wished very much that this had not been said because everyone seemed to agree so that the moment of choice became something more significant than it should have been, even though Randall was still grinning.

'It *is* obvious, isn't it?' he said, as he reached for Summer's mug and weighed it in his hand—practical, sturdy, big, the kind of mug you'd have in the galley of a smallish boat, its colour reminiscent of a warm, tropical ocean. 'So who is it that understands me so well?'

'Summer, of course,' came a chorus of four voices.

'Summer. . .' he echoed, and their eyes met.

'Just a lucky guess,' she said, smiling briefly and then turning away so that no one would see how hot she had grown.

'No, not at all. Very perceptive, actually, *I* think,' said Steve earnestly.

'But you're the only one without a new mug now,' Randall said quietly to her a moment later as the group broke up. Patients were beginning to arrive for their appointments and Lesley and Imelda still had things to do.

'I'll manage,' Summer answered him, making herself very busy with patient files. She *didn't* want to be close to him. She was already far too aware of him and hadn't needed that game with the mugs to remind her how well she knew him beneath the awful distance that separated them now.

'I'll buy you one,' he offered.

'You don't have to.'

'I want to.'

He seemed to want more, but now was not the time. He recognised the fact with apparent reluctance, she with relief, and she made very certain that she had changed into street clothes and got away while he was still with his last patient. He had said that he loved her. He had definitely despised her, although perhaps he no longer did. Was she going to forgive him for that?

But she wasn't destined to escape entirely, it seemed. John was waiting for her in the car park, restless and agitated, with his car parked in front of the two doctors' vehicles, blocking their exit.

'Come with me to Rose Beach,' he said. 'I've got things to do there, but we can talk on the way. Have dinner afterwards, if you like.'

'Talk?'

'You've got to convince Macleay that I'm ready for the pump!'

She was beside him in the car now, not quite knowing how she had got there but realising with those last words of his that she needed to be here.

'Why is it so important to you, John?' she asked him. 'It gives you great control, sure, but it's tough to use because it requires a huge amount of discipline and care in self-monitoring.'

'Which I've shown that I can do over the past couple of weeks.'

'I think Randall would want months of commitment before he'd be convinced it was the right thing. Please don't go chasing the idea as if it was a miracle cure, John!'

'I'm not.' Pressing his foot to the accelerator, he put on a rebellious spurt of speed—which wasn't much on Bermuda's slow, winding roads. 'Don't you understand, Summer? I need something to offer Alex. You were right, I love her too much to let her go. It's been killing me.

I've been a wreck until I realised I had to take *action.* I feel bad about using you in the way I did, but—'

'It's all right, John. There was that on both sides—the way I was feeling about my parents back then.'

'—I want to feel that I can go to Alex now with something concrete as proof that I'm getting my life back and I've got something to give her. I haven't had to work for much in my life. If I could work on this—get it right, get that optimum control—I'd be able to win her.'

'Oh, John, don't you think she's already won? She'd come to you in a minute if you said the word, even if you were at death's door.'

'No,' he said stubbornly. 'I won't have her on those terms.'

He meant it, and as he drove in silence Summer started to wonder if he was right. He'd never had to earn his place in the Wave Crest hotel chain. And his first response to his diabetes had been destructive, self-deluding and immature. Was this the chance he really needed to prove himself?

They were turning up the long drive to the Wave Crest Rose Beach resort when she said to him slowly, 'All right, John. I'll talk to Randall about it if you'd like me to.'

'Thanks, Summer. I can't tell you how much I appreciate that! Will you meet me for dinner in half an hour—once I've dealt with some business in the personnel office?'

'Sure, if you think I'm dressed for it.' She glanced down doubtfully at her simple navy linen-blend skirt and cream blouse.

'You're fine. And you're with me—you could be wearing a leather thong bikini and they'd have to let you in, if I said so.' It was an arrogant and rather young-sounding boast, but she forgave it quickly, and he disappeared into the hotel, leaving her to go for a walk in the lush, landscaped surrounds.

Before she could even decide which way to go, though, Maya Giangrande emerged from the main entrance and hailed her. 'Lovely to see you!'

'Yes, I—I'm having dinner with John.' Suddenly she felt awkward about it, the more so when she caught the glint of approval in Maya's eye.

'You are?' Maya came forward eagerly, her usual abrupt manner softening a little. 'Then you're rekindling things? That's so good! I thought he'd been looking better lately. He had been so low, thinking that you couldn't face life with his diabetes, but if you've come to realise that you can, after all—'

'Oh, no, Maya, you've got it all wrong!' Summer interrupted desperately. 'It wasn't his diabetes. You see, it was never me at all. Never me he really wanted, I mean. It's always been Alex Page, and *her* reaction to his disease that he couldn't trust.'

'Alex?' Maya echoed blankly.

'Yes, don't you remember? You told me yourself how strong their relationship had been, but then came the onset of his diabetes and he was so sure that she wouldn't be able to handle it that he didn't even give her the chance—didn't think it was fair to inflict it on her.'

'Hell, and I thought it was you. I even told Dr Macleay—' She stopped and gave a little laugh. 'I've experienced rejection myself because of my disease so perhaps it's a conclusion I jump to too readily! *I* decided in the end just to do without love rather than take the risk. I wasn't the marrying type, anyway. If John wants Alex, though, what is he waiting for? The girl is pining for him. I was over at our Bahamas resort last week and she's a wreck!'

'He's waiting till he can prove to her that he's got

good control,' Summer said, feeling winded by what Maya had said.

It was clear, now, why Randall had got the wrong idea about her and John. Maya carried conviction, too, with that brisk manner of hers. No wonder he had believed her without question! But perhaps it was too late to know this now. Fences so badly broken were hard to mend.

'That's ridiculous!' Maya was saying. 'Alex wouldn't want that. She wants him now, under any circumstances. What a mess it all is!'

'Yes, it is,' Summer agreed. 'An awful mess!'

Only she wasn't thinking of John and Alex at all.

Olivewood House was manicured and dressed up to perfection from the lawns that swept down to Castle Harbour to the collection of art deco mirrors in the dining-room. In this same dining-room, and in three other reception rooms linked by open archways, tables were laid for 122 guests, and Lesley had told the caterers to expect up to five times that number at the outdoor garden party later in the day.

The diabetes care centre's manager had been short-tempered and frantic all Friday, as obsessive as any bride with a huge wedding to organise. Flowers for the tables, place cards, guest speaker, marquee, volunteer co-ordination, contingency plan in case of rain. 'This is going to be our best fund-raiser yet.' But today no one would suspect from Lesley's face and manner what a lot of work had gone into organising the event.

'Good, Summer, you're here,' she said, tossing her head to flick strands of frosted blonde hair off her forehead. 'I've put you down to put the place cards on the tables. Here's the master plan and *don't* get it wrong, will you, my dear, because there are at least four couples coming who have a long-standing dislike of four *other* couples, and won't contribute a cent beyond the luncheon price if they're put at the same table—do you see what I mean?'

She smiled, patted Summer on the shoulder and hurried off to direct the roping-off of Olivewood's private rooms. John's parents, Vincent and Anna Giangrande, had wisely taken themselves off to New York for the weekend, leaving John to represent the family and liaise with the centre staff. Summer took the seating plan and the bundle of place cards, already ordered by table, and set to work.

About halfway through she came to her own name as the centre's staff had each been allocated a different table, and were under strict orders to help conversation flow smoothly until the guest speaker took the floor during dessert and coffee. Randall's name appeared on the diagram of the adjacent table, and she was just laying the card by his plate when she heard Lesley greet him.

'Randall! You're late! But now that I look at you I can see why. You look gorgeous. And I'm going to make the sexist assumption that as a man you'll know about electrical whatnots. You can check that the microphone is working and the speakers in each room.'

'I thought there was only one speaker,' came Randall's voice, very seriously. Summer hadn't dared to look up at him yet, and was studying her seating plan with unfocused eyes.

She had been so aware of him yesterday at work, not knowing whether to be glad or sorry that their paths had crossed so little. She needed to speak to him on John's behalf, but wanted to wait for the right moment. And there was a slow, creeping sense that he was waiting too, not angry any more but very watchful—wanting to know how she felt. She had caught his eyes on her once or twice, only to find that he had turned quickly away as soon as she looked in his direction.

'Yes, I mean *loud*speaker, amplifier or whatever you

call it.' Today Lesley was far too busy to realise when she was being teased. 'So we can *hear* the speaker. That is, the one speaker who's going to speak. You know, Rick Blair.'

'Got it,' Randall said, still straight-faced.

He came into the largest of the reception rooms, where Summer was at work, just as she came to Rick Blair's place card. The dais where the man would stand to speak was just behind her, and he would be seated nearby during the meal—at Randall's table.

Randall looked, as Lesley had said, gorgeous. There was really no other word for it. He wore a pale grey suit, and a shirt that was whiter than the catering firm's best china. His freshly washed hair was its usual dark, silver-threaded helmet, and a little sunburn from his most recent sail had mellowed into the lightest tan. Summer felt her knees go weak as he approached, skirting the tables with his usual lazy, loping stride until he reached her.

'Hi. . .' A hand brushed her shoulder, making the silk of her turquoise dress slip against her skin. Then he had passed by before she even had a chance to respond to his casual greeting.

Respond? Her body had responded, all right! Her skin burned where his hand had been and it sent a frisson of awareness radiating all through her. He seemed oblivious, which was all to the good. He had already plugged in the microphone cord which snaked behind the dais.

There was something about him, though—a return to the Randall that had been missing over the past few weeks. She loved the change but didn't dare to think about what it might mean.

She was looking forward to Rick Blair's speech, and she was sure that Randall would be too. The American was an adventurer by profession, and had chalked up half a dozen incredible feats—from ballooning the length of the Andes to deep-sea diving beneath Arctic ice. His exploits had been featured on television and in magazines, and he had just completed his third book. The fact that he had been an insulin-dependent diabetic since the age of eight was just one more challenge to a man who clearly thrived on challenges of every kind.

Stopping her work for a moment, she watched Randall. He was taping the microphone cord down now so that no one tripped on it. There was a ripping sound as he pulled a length of heavy black electrical tape from the thick roll, then he slashed it off with the glinting blade of his pocket-knife. Typical of Randall Macleay—to carry a Swiss Army knife in the pocket of that expensive-looking suit!

'You must be looking forward to sitting near Rick Blair,' Summer said carefully.

'Yes, he sounds like an interesting man,' was the equally careful reply. 'I suggested him to Lesley as a speaker several months ago, and it took a lot of work to chase him up. Lesley didn't think he'd be interested, but when I got on the phone and promised to take him out in *Aquamarine* for some good diving he couldn't resist. We're leaving at the crack of dawn tomorrow, and probably won't get back in until midnight.'

His manner was natural, casual. . .

I don't know what's happening between us, she thought miserably. He doesn't seem angry any more. I—I don't think I am either. If it really was just some awful misunderstanding because of what Maya said. . . Did he believe me the other day when I said that John's diabetes wasn't an issue?

She almost marched up to him then and there to have it out with him, but the timing wasn't right. For a moment it had seemed as if they were alone together, but of course they weren't. In the big kitchen the caterers were noisily at work, unpacking or preparing their vast quantities of food. Steve ducked his head in at the door to ask, 'Seen Lesley?' and the latter pounced on him before the words were fairly out of his mouth.

'Now, your next job, Steve. . .'

John came in and approached Lesley a moment later as well. 'All the lockable rooms are locked now. I'll hang onto the keys, if you don't mind.'

'Thanks. It really is so generous of your parents—'

He cut her off with a handsome smile and a magnanimous wave as he caught sight of Summer. He came straight up to her, imperiously taking her attention from the place cards by simply pulling them from her and dropping them carelessly on the table. He took her hands in his. 'Have you spoken to Dr Macleay yet?'

'There hasn't been a chance, John. You can see how busy we are, and it was the same yesterday too, setting up signs in the grounds, organising rosters of helpers for the garden party. . .'

'Don't you see how this is eating me?'

'Yes, I do, but—'

'Here, if I do these place cards. . . Now, what's Macleay doing? He's finished with the speaker system. Please, Summer—! You're the perfect person—tactful, informed, beguiling—and we've opened our house for this event, for heaven's sake!'

There it was again, that mixture of charm, flattery and unquestioning entitlement that had both won her and lost her again several months ago.

'All right, John,' she answered helplessly. 'I'll see if I can find somewhere private.'

He thrust the keys at her. 'This gold one opens the conservatory.'

'OK, but. . .'

'Just lock it up afterwards. Now, these place cards. . .'

He was still shuffling them distractedly in his hand and getting them quite out of order, when Maya swept in, looking her usual sophisticated self in tailored nutmeg-brown linen.

'Here he is, Alex,' she said, her voice carrying clearly, and just behind her was Alex Page, the immaculate impression given by her pink silk suit belied by nervousness and a weight loss around her face that even expert make-up could not hide.

'Alex!' John said.

The place cards fell in a sweeping fan all over the floor and Lesley froze with an anguished hiss. Randall was warily transfixed, dangling the roll of electrical tape in his hands as if it was his coffee-mug, but—out of sight in the next room—Steve was humming an old Beatles song very dreadfully, unaware that anything was going on at all.

'Alex. . .'

They crossed the room to each other. 'Maya phoned me on Thursday,' the lovely blonde said. 'How could you think your illness would matter to me, John? How could you shut me out like that?'

'I couldn't see you in that role. I didn't want to put you . . .*force* you into it. But if you're prepared to, if you want me—'

'Of course I *want* you! I love you! I could *kill* you for hurting me like you have these past months!'

They left the room together, oblivious to anyone else. There was a slightly stunned silence.

'Well, that was easy,' Maya said briskly. 'Now, is there anything I can do?'

'Well, since it doesn't look as if we'll be seeing much more of John today. . .' Lesley began.

Summer bent down to gather up the place cards and realised that she still had the bunch of Olivewood House keys in her hands. She straightened, looked at them blankly and then saw that Randall was watching her.

'John gave them to me,' she explained vaguely. 'He wanted me to press his case to you about using an insulin pump so he would feel able to offer himself to Alex again, but I don't suppose it matters now.'

'Doesn't look that way,' he agreed. 'We'll work towards it if he wants to so badly. But what about you, Summer?'

He was close to her now—close enough for her to be fully aware of him in the way that she had been almost from the beginning, and she was helpless to disguise his effect on her.

'What *about* me?' she managed.

'Please pick up the rest of those place cards, Summer,' Lesley wailed as she approached, 'before someone tramples them.'

Then she stopped in her tracks and looked from Summer to Randall and back again. 'On second thoughts, whatever was going on between the two of you a few weeks ago seems to have had a relapse. Go and get it out of your systems, would you, please? And I'll do the place cards myself. All I ask, Randall, is that you remember to come back in time to give your speech and introduce Rick Blair.'

'I will, Lesley, I promise,' he said, his humility belied by the glint in his eye. 'I'm sorry about this. . .'

'I'm not. It may improve your mood. Just get it over with!'

'Now, what best describes the way I feel at the moment?' Randall mused on a guilty growl as he and Summer skulked obediently from the room to head in the direction of the conservatory, the key to which was now growing hot and damp in Summer's hand.

'Like a child who's been caught bringing a live frog to the dinner table and promptly been told to go and put it back in the garden this minute,' Summer suggested immediately.

'How did you know?'

'Because I feel the same way.'

'Well, are we going to?'

'Going to what?'

'Put the frog back in the—? Actually, that could be taken in a rather suggestive way—*Summer*?'

'Yes, Randall?'

They had reached the large, lush conservatory, and this was all suddenly far too important for humour.

'I've been so angry with you. It feels so good *not* to be...' He said it against her mouth, and she lifted her face to his to return his melting kiss. 'Oh, God, does it feel good!'

He drank the taste of her hungrily, leaving her quite breathless. A part of her still wanted to protest...to thrash this all out before she gave in to her physical need...but a bigger part of her just couldn't care less and returned in full the touch of his lips—drowning in him, melting against him, legs weak, heart pounding, spirits singing.

'I got it all wrong and I'm deeply sorry,' he said in a low voice. 'If you forgive me it's more than I deserve.'

'I do forgive you,' she told him, her hands shaping the strong flesh of his back as she listened to his heartbeat against her ear. 'I'd be cutting off my nose to spite my face if I didn't. I—I love you, Randall. I just don't quite understand how you could get such a mistaken idea. I know it was partly Maya's fault...'

'It was *my* fault,' he insisted, 'for immediately believing her, instead of realising just how much her angle on you and John was coloured by her own diabetes. I do tend to get up in arms over any prejudice against my patients. You don't know how much I wished John *wasn't* my patient! But it was what you said out sailing on that last

Saturday, too, that I couldn't forget. ''I wouldn't have made a good wife to him. People think they can handle it, but then find that they can't.'' Those aren't the exact words, I expect, but pretty close. . .'

'I meant the role of a rich man's wife,' she said, looking up into the heated depth of his blue eyes. 'Randall, I don't even like fancy restaurants much. It would have been a constant effort for me to live John's lifestyle, schmoozing with important hotel guests, being seen at all the best Bermuda functions.'

'Then what I'm offering you doesn't sound too humble?'

'What *are* you offering me? You haven't actually said. . .'

He kissed her from her ear to her neck and back again, then said against her mouth, 'Everything I wanted to offer you that night at my place when I foolishly let you escape without spending the night. My heart, my hand, my boat, my house. . .'

'In descending order of importance?'

'Just about. And a ring, too, although not as *big*, I'm afraid, as what you're used to.' A smile played on his face, and she could return it at last.

'I expect I'll cope,' she answered him drily.

'Speaking of which, I wonder if Lesley is.' This conservatory was tucked away, opening off a guest suite at the opposite end of the house. Listening, they could hear nothing of the preparations going on.

'Oh, I imagine Maya's been roped in,' Summer suggested, assuaging any guilt at the thought of her patient's efficiency.

'Is that a little hint that you'd like to stay here a bit longer?'

'Yes, please! But only if you kiss me,' she told him sternly.

'What an onerous proviso,' he murmured. 'But I think I can manage it.'

And he did, very thoroughly, with every touch of his lips and hands promising all the passion that would blaze between them from this night onwards.

MILLS & BOON®

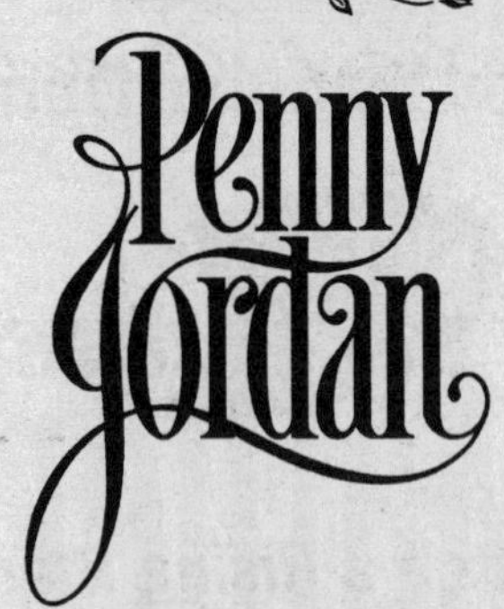

A PERFECT FAMILY

But shocking revelations and heartache lie just beneath the surface of their charmed lives

Mills & Boon are proud to bring you this thrilling family saga from international bestselling author, Penny Jordan.

Long-held resentments and jealousies are reawakened when three generations of the Crighton family gather for a special birthday celebration—revealing a family far from perfect underneath!

Available: September 1997 Price: £4.99 (384pp)

*** 50p off A Perfect Family ***

See September Mills & Boon books.
Redeemable against Retail Purchase only.